IT'S ALL DONE WITH MIRRORS. . . .

Robert Wilson knew he was living in a book. He had discovered this when somebody showed him the book in question. It was called *Great Short Stories* and was by some Yank named Hemingway. And there he was, Robert Wilson, playing a featured role in the very first story, "The Short Happy Life of Francis Macomber."

Then Wilson discovered that he was in *another* book, but changed in totally arbitrary ways that verged on surrealism. This book was a bit of tommyrot and damned filth called *The Universe Next Door* and he was, in fact, both inside it and outside it, being both author of it and a character in it.

Books by Robert Anton Wilson

The Cosmic Trigger
Masks of the Illuminati
Schrödinger's Cat: The Trick Top Hat
Schrödinger's Cat: The Universe Next Door
Schrödinger's Cat III: The Homing Pigeons

Published by POCKET BOOKS

Robert Anton Wilson

SCHRÖDINGER'S CAT III

The Homing Pigeons

PUBLISHED BY POCKET BOOKS NEW YORK

Another *Original* publication of POCKET BOOKS

POCKET BOOKS, a Simon & Schuster division of
GULF & WESTERN CORPORATION
1230 Avenue of the Americas, New York, N.Y. 10020

ISBN: 0-671-82119-9

First Pocket Books printing June, 1981

10 9 8 7 6 5 4 3 2 1

POCKET and colophon are trademarks of Simon & Schuster.

Printed in the U.S.A.

to
Harold Garfinkle
Carlos Castaneda
and
Richard de Mille
"Greetings on all three points of the triangle"

CAVEAT LECTOR

The three volumes of the *Schrödinger's Cat* series can be read in any order desired.

That is, this volume can be read before or after the volumes called *The Universe Next Door* and *The Trick Top Hat,* or between them.

These volumes may also be read before or after the three volumes of the *Illuminatus* trilogy and before or after *Masks of the Illuminati.*

The author wishes to thank Dr. Blake Williams for permission to quote material from his conversations, letters, diaries, etc., intended for publication in Dr. Williams' five-volume study, *Quantum Physics and Neuro-Linguistics.*

Everything here is true. Einstein, Schrödinger, the Mad Fishmonger, the Invisible Hand, Unistat, and even the Tooth Fairy are real. Fortunately for us, however, they do not exist in this space-time continuum, but in the universe next door.

There is a glossary at the back for those who may find some of the quantum physics a bit heavy.

CAVE CANEM

The
First
Loop

All Cretans are liars.
> —Empedocles the Cretan

The President of the United States is not a crook.
> —The President of the United States

Death to all fanatics!
> —Malaclypse the Younger

THE UNIVERSE WILL SURPRISE US

Jen fa Ti: Ti fa T'sien;
T'sien fa Tao: Tao fa tzu-jan.

—Lao-Tse, *Tao Te Ching*

Tall, skinny palm trees, twisted to bizarre angles by dozens of Florida hurricanes, stood black against a cinnamon-streaked sky as the sun rose majestically in the west.

"We stop here," Mavis said, as he had known she would: as was, perhaps, inevitable now.

This must be the Gulf of Mexico, Dashwood thought. They could now load him with chains and drop him *in the drink,* as criminals said, letting him sink slowly down amid the sharks and barracudas, down where, after the sharks were finished, the King Crabs would pick what was left on his bones, down, down, down, full fathom five.

And, as was inevitable now, Mavis motioned him out of the car, stepping out behind him (still holding that damned tommy gun, as if quietly toying with it) like the ghoats in hammelts.

"We wait here," she said. "The others go back."

"What are we waiting for?" Dashwood asked.

"Don't be a dummy, George. We rescued you, remember? Like the gauds in ambers."

Dashwood took a deep breath, counting to ten. "Why do you keep calling me George? You know my name is Frank, damn it."

Mavis opened her eyes wide, pretending astonishment. "You really don't remember," she said sadly.

A woodpecker landed wearily on the nearest palm, as if he had flown more missions than Yossarian and never intended to go up again.

"I'm Frank Dashwood," he said. "Dr. Francis R. Dash-

11

wood. I'm a member of the American Psychiatric Association. I'm in *Who's Who. Goddamn it,*" he added, irrelevantly but heatedly.

"You're George Dorn," she said. "You work for *Confrontation* magazine. Your boss is named Justin Case."

"Oh, balls," Dashwood said.

The woodpecker turned his head, as perhaps was sure to happen now, and watched them suspiciously, like a paranoid old man.

And Dashwood noticed, as for the first time, an unfinished building on the beach, probably a new condo, with girders going off at strange cubist angles. Skeletons in hard hats stood frozen like statues, and a giant squid reached up from the ocean to wrap its tentacles around the pylons.

The sun was as hot as Gunga Din's loincloth.

A vine-colored plaque at the gate said:

FATALITY INC.
Muss. S. Sine, President
S. Muss Sine, Vice-President

"If I'm George Dorn," he said finally, "why do I have this deep-seated longtime delusion that I'm Frank Dashwood?"

"We're in Maybe-time here," Mavis said. "You know: 'In addition to a Yes and a No, the universe contains a Maybe.' You've heard that, I'm sure. It's hard to keep track of social fictions out here, and personal identity is just a social fiction. So you've lost your ego for a few minutes and grabbed hold of another one. That's how you created this imaginary Frank Fernwood."

"Dashwood," he corrected automatically.

"Going home from here isn't easy," Mavis said, still toying with the tommy gun. "Some people never find their way back. That's why you must let go out of this Frank Fernwood delusion."

"It's Dashwood, damn it, *Dashwood!*"

"Fernwood, Dashwood," she said impatiently. "Deep down you know you're George Dorn."

"You are a fruitcake, Mavis. Why did you rescue me from that jail, anyway?"

"You're wanted," she said simply.

"By whom?"

"Hagbard Celine."

"And who is Hagbard Celine?" They had reached the cabana and were standing beside it, glaring at each other like two chess masters who each suspect that they have wandered into some idiotic permutation of the Ourang-Outan opening. The woodpecker turned his head, probably a bit puzzled himself, and sized them up with the other eye.

"You'll know when you meet him, George." ["Frank," he shouted. "George," she repeated firmly.] "For now it's enough that he wanted us to get you out of Bad Ass Jail."

"And why the hell does Hagbard Chelling . . ." ["Celine," she corrected.] ". . . Celine, then, why the hell does Hagbard Celine want to see me?"

"Why anything?" Mavis asked rhetorically. "Why sky, why oceans, why people? Jen fa Ti: Ti fa T'sien: T'sien fa Tao: Tao fa tzu-jan."

"Oh, *coitus*," Dashwood said, avoiding crudity. "Don't give me obscurities in Cantonese at this hour."

"Men are created by earth, earth is created by the universe, the universe is created by Nature's Process, and Nature's Process just happened," Mavis translated.

Dashwood was not going to get involved in aleotoric cosmologies. "So Hagbard Celine just happened," he said. "And he just happened to want me out of Bad Ass Jail. And you just happen to like busting into jails with tommy guns and taking prisoners out. This is the silliest damned routine I ever heard."

"Well," Mavis said, grinning wickedly, "I also just happen to like you. In fact, I've had the Whites for you ever since I broke into the cell back in Bad Ass and caught you Lourding off."

"Don't talk dirty," he said. "It's not becoming to a young woman your age, and it's getting silly and old-fashioned. It makes you sound like a refugee from the 1960s."

"Nonsense," Mavis said. "It gets you excited. It always gets men excited to hear women talk like this. Do you know how I felt when I saw you there on the bunk with your Rehnquist in your hand? It made my Feinstein go all warm and mushy inside, George."

"Frank," he said one more time. "And I don't have the

13

Whites for you. Women wtih tommy guns don't turn me on at all."

"Are you sure?" Mavis asked provocatively. "I'll bet I could make your Rehnquist stand up if I really tried." She opened her trenchcoat and he could see her magnificent Brownmillers bulging through her tight sweater. He had to admit they were a fine, firm pair of Brownmillers—"a pair you could hang your hat on," as an Irishman had once said —but he was not going to be tempted. This was all too weird.

"I've had a lot of tension since raiding the jail," Mavis went on, slipping the trenchcoat to the sand. "I really need a good Potter Stewart, George. Wouldn't you like to Potter Stewart me? Wouldn't you like to lie on the sand and stick your great big pulsating Rehnquist up into my warm, moist Feinstein?"

"This is ridiculous."

"Listen, George," Mavis went on intensely. "When I was young I decided to save myself for a man who completely meets the criteria of my value system. That's when I was reading Ayn Rand, you see. But then I realized I could get awfully horny waiting for him to come along. You'll have to do."

How can you keep the facts clear and sharp-edged when this happens? "You really want me to Potter Stewart you right now on a public beach in broad daylight?" he asked, feeling like a fool.

The woodpecker went to work above them just then, banging away like a Rock drummer. Dashwood remembered from Nutley High School:

The woodpecker pecked on the outhouse door;
He pecked and he pecked till his pecker was sore

"George, you're too serious. Don't you know how to play? Did you ever think that life is maybe a game? The world is a toy, George. I'm a toy. You conjured me out of your fantasies while you were Lourding-off in that jail cell last night. I'm a magic voodoo doll. You can do anything you want with me."

Dashwood shook his head. "I can't believe you. The way you're talking—it's not real."

"I always talk this way when I'm horny. It so happens that at such tender moments I'm more open to the vibrations from outer space. George, is the Tooth Fairy real? Is the thought of the Tooth Fairy a real thought? How is it different from the mental picture of my Brownmillers that you get when you imagine you can look right through my sweater? Does the fact that you can think of Potter Stewarting me and I can think of Potter Stewarting you mean that we *are* going to Potter Stewart? Or is the universe going to surprise us?"

"The universe is going to surprise *you*," Dashwood said. "I don't trust women with tommy guns who rave about Tooth Fairies and vibrations from outer space. I'm getting the hell out of here." He started to walk away.

"Listen, George," Mavis said earnestly. "You are about to walk into a completely different universe, one you might not like at all. Every quantum decision creates a whole new space-time manifold . . ."

"Oh, bullburger," he said, before she could go any further with that gibberish.

"You damned fool! You're walking out on the greatest adventure of our century!" She was almost shouting now. "Atlantis! Illumination! Leviathan! Hagbard Celine!"

Dashwood kept going.

"You asshole!" she screamed. "You're about to miss *the best Steinem-Job of your life.*"

He almost turned then, but this was all too bizarre for him. He continued down the asphalt road grimly, ignoring the Yellow Submarine that was beginning to surface offshore.

Blake Williams galloped past him suddenly, riding a whorse with no wife and no mustache. He was Lassie (who was really a male dog in drag), but he was also Dashwood's father. Like the Gutmanhammett.

Then Furbish Lousewart came out of the lavatory wearing a laboratory smock. "The masses are female," he sneered, drawing a rotary saw out of his toolbox depository. He methodically began sawing off Dashwood's head. "Give me head!" he screamed. "The whiteness of the wall! Gothin haven, annette colp us! Give me head!"

And then Linda Lovelace was there, with Dracula's old red-lined cape, starting to suck him, starting to suck the purity of essense from him, biting down hard hard hard, a blood-smeared mouth with canine fangs.

And he woke up.

He looked at the alarm clock blearily, still haunted by fangs and blood. Six-fifty-eight; the alarm would go off in two minutes.

I am Frank Dashwood. All that other was just a dream.

He depressed the alarm switch and put his naked feet on the cold floor, so he would not roll over and dream he was going to work.

Fangs and blood. Why do people see such films? Weird species, we are.

Dr. Dashwood staggered to the shower. White tile, white on white: the whiteness of the wall. Vibrations from outer space, she said. Not too hot, now: careful. Ah, that's good. Watch that it doesn't heat up too fast, though. Fangs and blood: average person has seen one hundred, maybe two hundred, of those films. Hundreds of hours of horror grooves in the brain: neurological masochism. *YEEEEEE-EEEEEEEEEEEEEEE!*

He turned the hot-water spigot down quickly. Always does that: starts tepid and then boils you.

He leaped from the shower and began toweling. Oral sadism: she looked good enough to eat, we say. Little Red Riding Hood. Eatupus complex.

Dashwood surveyed his features in the mirror, combing his hair. As the world sees me: this not unhandsome, definitely nervous, middle-aged face.

Radio will bring me all the way back. Try KKHI, maybe catch some Vivaldi. Dashwood's Law: whenever you turn on KKHI, they're either playing Vivaldi or will play Vivaldi within fifteen minutes.

De de dum de dum de dee
De de dum de dum de dum dum dum

Sounds more like Bach. Wait: listen:

> De de drum de drum de DRUM
> Drum drum de droom de de
>   Wheeeee dumb dee!

And that was the Concerto for Harp *by Jan Ze-lenka. And now the news. In Bad Ass, Texas, School Superintendent B. S. Curve was murdered last night by a bomb attached to the starter of his automobile. Superintendent Curve had been under attack by local clergy and the John Birch Society for proposing the teaching of the metric system in schools. In Washington, President K——*

Dashwood snapped the radio off irritably. Whenever you want to hear some pleasant music, they break for the news. Ah, well: time to head for the office, anyway.

De de dum de dum de dee . . . Where the hell did I put the key? Oh, yes: alarm clock, next to. Dum de de: sure sounded like Bach at first. Dum drum de dee! Really bounced along, music of that period. Baroque.

He started his car.

Crrrrumph rumph rumph.

Oh, damn. Try again.

Crrrrrrrrrrumph rumph a zoom.

Dashwood pulled out into the traffic. Always fails to ignite first time. Dum dum de. Zelenka, he said. Who the hell was Zelenka? Same period as Bach, I'm sure.

Dr. Dashwood turned onto Van Ness and headed for Orgasm Research: da dum da dum da *dreee!*

And drove straight into an entirely different kind of novel.

GALACTIC ARCHIVES:

Although generally regarded as one of the two or three real masterpieces produced during humanity's primitive, terrestrial stage, *The Homing Pigeons* is admittedly a somewhat strange and often puzzling saga.

Some of the obscurities in the text are due, of course, to the mere passage of time and the loss of records. We will never know, for instance, which of the ancient Bard's

17

heroes and heroines were real people and which were fictitious characters invented by him.

However, serious scholars are now agreed that the Bard himself was probably fictitious. We will never know the real name of the author of these immortal pages; we can only be sure that he (or she, if one believes the Butlerian theory) was not the same Robert Anton Wilson who later composed or collected the legends in *The Trick Top Hat*. (An earlier, now totally lost work, *The Universe Next Door*, was certainly not composed by either of these Bards, but by a relative named Robert Anson Wilson.)

We can be sure also that no such place as Unistat ever existed, although the sublime myth-maker of this epic undoubtedly based Unistat on his own republic or city-state, which was probably called something like United States of Amnesia or United States of Armorica and may be identical with the Armorica where Tristan found Isolde of the White Hands.

Certainly, too, the politics of Unistat could not be based on real events, even in those barbaric and bloody days. We must suspect our Author of indulging in satire at times, especially when dealing with the dread F.B.I., the eldritch C.I.A., and other Powers of Darkness.

The most puzzling details of this saga occur in scenes involving sexual activity. It is believed that there is a simple explanation for these enigmas. The Bard, we now believe, grew up in the generation immediately following the epoch-making breakthroughs in erotic realism of such Terran geniuses—known to us only in legend, since their works are lost—as T. H. Lawrence, Norman Miller, and Henry Mailer. With such Teachers, our present author felt it natural to write of such matters in the simple, straightforward language of the day; but, unfortunately for him, the pendulum had meanwhile swung backward toward puritanism. Trapped between the feeling that honest writing was best, and the certainty that such realism would bring opprobrium down upon him, the wily Bard elected to resort to a kind of code.

According to Professor Jubelum, the outstanding authority on the weirdities of late, pre-Migration Terran literature, the strange words used for sexual references in this Romance are all proper names. Evidently, the malicious Bard decided to escape the wrath of the puritans by using their *names* for sexual parts and functions, on the grounds that they could hardly regard their own appelatives as "dirty," "obscene," or "sexist."

Such were the constrictions with which servants of the Muse had to struggle in primitive times.

THE MAD ARAB

Qol: Hua Allahu achad; Allahu Assamad; lam yalid walam yulad; walam yakun lahu kufwan achad.

—*Al Qoran*

One day earlier and three thousand miles due East, Bonita ("Bonny") Benedict, a popular columnist for the New York *News-Times-Post-Herald-Dispatch-Express-Mirror-Eagle*, sat down to write her daily stream-of-consciousness. According to her usual procedure, Bonny began by flipping through her notebook. This usually served to fructify her imagination, but that day proved rather sterile. Items which had already been used were crossed out with large X's and what was left was weary, stale, flat, and unprofitable. There was literally nothing timely or exciting enough for a lead.

Bonny was only stumped for a minute; then she remembered the ancient maxim of the great pioneer of modern journalism, Charles Foster Hearst: "If there isn't any news, invent some."

Ms. Benedict, whose hair would have been gray if she hadn't decided it was more chic to bleach it pure platinum-white, had lasted in the news game for forty years. She did not lack the faculty of imagination.

Bonny inserted a fresh sheet in the typewriter and began at once, trusting her years of experience to guide her. What emerged was:

Who is the man in Hong Kong who looks exactly like Lee Harvey Oswald? Believe it or not, darlings, that question is causing a lot of excitement among the members of the new Senate Committee on Congressional Committees on Assassinations. In case you forgot, they're the ones who are trying to find out why the various Congressional Committees on Assassinations couldn't find out anything. What they're asking each other is: Could the man in Hong Kong really be Oswald? And, if so, who was the double that got shot in Dallas? Doesn't it make your heads swim???

That was what was known as a fail-safe item. If (as was likely) the Senate Committee simply ignored it rather than fan the flames of rumor, many readers would believe it on the grounds that it had been printed and not denied. If, on the other hand, the Committee did deny it, even more people would believe it. A 1981 psychological survey had shown that sixty-seven percent of the population experienced uncertainty, indecision, suspicion, or downright paranoia whenever they saw the words "government denial" in print.

Bonny went on to use up the not-totally dreary items in her notebook, jazzing each one enough to give it a coat of sparkle, or at least of tinsel. But she still needed a zinger for the closing. She followed the sage advice of the prophet Hearst one more time and wrote:

Wasn't that Furbish Lousewart of the Purity of Ecology Party eating steak and drinking Manhattans (made with Southern Comfort, my dears!) at Sardi's last night? What would the Party regulars think of this flagrant disregard of P.O.E. principles?

Bonny, in her youth, had been a disciple of the famous feminist and psychologist, Alberta Einstein. It was Ms. Einstein, in her epoch-making *Neuro-Psychology*, who introduced the concept that every brain constructs a different "island-reality" from the billions of signals it receives every minute. This concept had revolutionized the social sciences and even led Heisenberg to propose a similar relativity principle in physics. Bonny knew that the P.O.E. people lived in an island-reality where eating meat and drinking fermented spirits were atrocities comparable to ax murder or Burgering in the well. This item would make them hopping mad.

A columnist's career depends on amusing most of her

readers most of the time and making some of them hopping mad some of the time.

The owner-publisher of the New York *News-Times*-&c was Polly Esther Doubleknit, relict of the late Dacron Doubleknit, the leisurewear king. When the leisurewear fad had peaked in the 1970s, Dacron had shrewdly used the cash flow to *"diversify,"* as his accountant called it. Engulf and Devour, his competitors called it. When he died, Dacron owned over a thousand retail stores coast to coast, a tapioca mine in Nutley, N.J. (a bad investment, that one, suggested by a plausible but Machiavellian midget), a large hunk of Canadian forestland, three South American governments (his leisurewear was thereafter made with very cheap labor), sixteen Congresspersons, three Senators, a shipyard in Yellow Springs, Ohio (suggested by Eva Gebloomenkraft), seven state legislatures together with four other whorehouses in Nevada, and the New York *News-Times*-u.s.w.

Dacron died of a heart attack at fifty-two, brought on by anxiety about the amount of political corruption he was involved in. Dacron did not *like* to bribe public officials and *hated* the size of the bribes they all wanted, because he had been raised a Presbyterian. Unfortunately for him, he lived in an age of Terminal Bureaucracy and there was absolutely no way, no matter how many lawyers he hired, to find out if his corporations were, in any given instance, in violation of the law. There were too many laws, and they were written in language that guaranteed maximum ambiguity all around, so that lawyers (who wrote the laws) could always get jobs proving that the laws meant Yes, if they were being paid to prove that, or that the laws meant No, if they were being paid to prove that. Dacron could never find out, for sure, whether he was the one businessman in the country operating one hundred percent legally all the time, or if he was in violation of so many statutes that he was subject to over a thousand years in prison; no two lawyers ever would agree about that. So Dacron bribed as many officials as possible to protect himself, and then gradually worried himself to death about the bribes being discovered someday.

Polly Esther, finding herself the heir of Dacron's far-raginous empire, quickly appointed professional executives to manage most of it; but she took over the newspaper personally. She was a fan of a TV show called "Lou Grant" and rather fancied herself as becoming another Mrs. Pynchon.

Mrs. Pynchon was the publisher of the paper on the "Lou Grant" show. She was tough enough to eat barbed wire and spit tacks, but she was also cool and elegant. Polly Esther wanted to be like that.

She also had a secret desire to be the other Mrs. Pynchon, the wife of the novelist. She had read one of Pynchon's novels once while dieting, and maybe she had used just a little bit too many of those diet pills, because she believed every word of it. She was still convinced that the baskets on the street saying W.A.S.T.E. meant We Await Silent Tristero's Empire.

Naturally, Polly Esther believed both of Bonny Benedict's fictions of the day. She had long suspected that both Oswald and Lousewart were agents of Silent Tristero's Empire.

Polly Esther was about forty-two but could easily pass for thirty-two. This was because she was very rich.

Once a year Polly Esther went to a ranch in Nevada which looked like a luxury motel and treated its guests like the inmates of a concentration camp. They fed Polly Esther on a diet that would barely sustain life and tasted horrible. They made her exercise several hours a day. A brutal staff insulted her, mocked her, bullied her, and got her back on her feet again, running, every time she thought she'd drop from exhaustion. They also shot her full of Gerovitol, methamphetamines, and vitamins three times a day. They charged her fifty-five hundred dollars.

Some of this actually had a slight effect on her body, but most of it was directed at her mind. She came out of this two-week ordeal, each year, convinced that she had suffered enough to *deserve* to be beautiful for another fifty weeks.

She was indeed beautiful, and had been a flaming red-head for so long that only a few people in Xenia, Ohio, remembered her as a dark-haired girl who had to leave town because of a scandal in the local Baptist church choir.

The robot who traveled under the name "Frank Sullivan" was in New York the next morning and saw Bonny Benedict's column. "Oh, Burger, Lourde, and corruption," he muttered, the newspaper trembling in his hands.

He immediately canceled his business in New York and hopped an orbital to Washington, where he leaped into a cab, sped to Naval Intelligence, and galloped into the office of Admiral Mounty ("Iron Balls") Babbit.

Babbit was in charge of "Dungeon and Dragon" operations, including the "Sullivan" matter; these were machinations so murky that they were not even known to those normally cleared for covert operations.

"How the holy Potter Stewart did she get hold of this?" pseudo-Sullivan demanded, waving Bonny Benedict's column.

Babbit stopped breathing for a minute as he read the Second Oswald item.

"Jesus and Mary Christ," he said finally, in a hollow tone. "The Briggsing Bryanting Frankel, she must have a source in the C.I.A. Those mother-Stewarting sons-of-bitches, they'll do anything to blow one of our operations."

This was typical of Old Iron Balls, as his men called him. He was convinced that everything malign emanated from Central Intelligence over in Alexandria. They spent all their time, he believed, plotting to discredit Naval Intelligence, and all because a high C.I.A. official had once caught him, Mounty Babbit, in an intimate moment with the C.I.A. man's mistress.

"Those bastards," he repeated in a tone as cold as official charity. "I'd like to blow that Burger-house in Alexandria off the face of the earth and every limp-wristed Briggsing Bryanting Harvard egghead in it."

But that was only one level of Old Iron Balls' mind—

the public level. Much deeper, he was already plotting various scenarios that resulted from the sudden deaths of Bonny Benedict or "Frank Sullivan."

Of course, Babbit did not for a moment contemplate assassination in the vulgar sense; there had been more than enough of that sort of thing back in the '60s and it had made all sorts of trouble for everybody in the Intelligence game. Babbit was guided by a maxim now universally accepted in the cloak-and-dagger business, although originally formulated by Beria of the NKVD: "Any damned fool can commit murder. Any halfway trained operative can arrange a convincing suicide. It takes an artist to manage an authentic natural death."

Pseudo-Sullivan had a larger than average share of E.S.P., as did many persons in the Intelligence game. "You know," he said casually, "I've left Certain Papers in a Certain Place to be opened in case of sudden death. . . ."

"Oh, you needn't worry about anything like that," Babbit said hastily. "Why, you're one of our most valuable um men. We wouldn't dream of . . ." Blah-blah-blah. It was a set speech, for occasions like this.

He was thinking of Bonny Benedict and of her publisher, that hoity-toity rich Frankel-Briggser, Polly Esther Double-knit.

The next fuse ignited by the Oswald-in-Hong-Kong story was in the frontal cortex of a balding, nervous man named Justin Case, who was living in a sociological treatise. That is, people made him so anxious that he shielded himself from them with a cocoon of words and concepts which had gradually become more real to him than the people were. He was a heavyweight Intellectual.

Justin Case had more Moral Concern than was good for a man. He worried about racism and sexism and imperialism and injustice and the general cussedness of his species; he agonized over each and every person on the planet who might be getting a raw deal; if you put enough martinis in him, he would start singing "Joe Hill" and "We Shall Overcome" and "Which Side are You On?" and other old Labor and Civil Rights songs.

Naturally, Case was the editor of a Liberal Magazine. The magazine was called *Confrontation* and had been started by a mad Arab named Joe Malik, who abandoned it in 1968 to enter a Trappist monastery. Malik had been traumatized by the Democratic Convention that year and told everybody he intended to spend the rest of his life in vehement and continuous prayer.

Malik left behind a note which still hung on the bulletin board at *Confrontation*. It said:

Qol: Hua Allahu achad; Allahu Assamad; lam yalid walam yulad; walam yakun lahu kufwan achad.

Nobody at *Confrontation* could read Arabic, but they all liked to stop and look at the note occasionally, wondering what it meant.

The stockholders had appointed Case to the editorship, after Malik retreated to the cloister, because Justin had as much righteous indignation as the mad Arab but was not so flaky.

By Spring 1984, Case had one hundred twenty bound volumes of books, articles, and press clippings about the J.F.K. assassination, since he was still Righteously Indignant about the palpably obvious cover-up involved in the *Warren Report*.

The day that pseudo-Sullivan wigged out over Bonny Benedict's contribution to the mythology of the assassination, Case calmly clipped that item and added it to his file.

Three-quarters of the other material in Case's file was also fictitious. One-third of this disinformation had been generated by Intelligence Agencies—domestic, foreign, and extraterrestrial—as covers or screens for their own activities in and around Dallas in 1963. Another third had been produced by sincere, dedicated, sometimes avid *conspiracy buffs*, weaving their own webs of confusion as they searched for the elusive truth. The last third had been created, like the Bonny Benedict item, by journalists following Hearst's advice about what to do when there was no news.

Anybody trying to find out "what *really* happened" from this collection of mythology would be so confused that the significant fact of the extraterrestrial intervention would never be apparent.

Case did not suspect any of this. He loved his J.F.K. file.

He was convinced that someday the crucial piece would come to him, he would insert it into the file, and the whole jigsaw would make sense.

He never realized that the one detail which gave everything away was that while Oswald was firing from the sixth-floor window he was also having a Coke on the second floor and mingling with the crowd in the street.

Like most liberals, Justin Case lacked imagination and never took seriously all the evidence of extraterrestrial activity on earth during the past forty years.

Case was currently having an affair with the Hollywood actress Carol Christmas.

Carol was renowned among the heterosexual male population for having the biggest Brownmillers since Jayne Mansfield; so far only women and a few Gay men had noticed that she could also act.

Carol had been married four times. She had had three abortions. Like other famous Beauties, she was *always* dieting, and, hence, a little bit high-strung. She was also a disciple of General E. A. Crowley, the eccentric English explorer who had discovered the North Pole and claimed there was a hole there leading down to the center of the Earth. Carol devoutly believed Crowley's yarn that there was a whole civilization down there, inside the Earth, run by green-skinnned women.

Carol believed this because she had a great artistic faith in the principle of balance. In her probability-continuum—in the series of quantum *eigen*states that had crystalized into her universe—the whole outside of the planet seemed to be run by white-skinned males. It was only fair that the inside should be run by green-skinned females.

Carol was having three other affairs at the same time as her *amour* with Justin Case. There was a hairdresser in Hollywood (bi, not Gay) who was very talented at Bryanting and Briggsing—two arts at which totally straight men, in Carol's opinion, were usually a bit clumsy. There was also François Loup-Garou, the painter, in Paris, who adored her madly, as only a painter can adore a woman. And there was a bitter but brilliant Black novelist in Chicago named Franklin Stuart.

There was also, in Hollywod along with the hairdresser, a certain rich producer; but that was not an *affair,* properly speaking, but a necessity of the marketplace.

Justin Case knew all about these other *amours;* after all, he read Bonny Benedict's column every day. Bonny kept the world informed about which celebrities were Potter Stewarting each other. She did this in a way that was perfectly clear to every reader but totally without any clear meaning in a court of law, in case somebody got irritated and tried to sue her. What she did was to write something like, "Hollywood sexpot Carol Christmas and Black novelist Frank Stuart are an item these days."

Everybody knew what "an item" meant.

When Bonny wrote that a couple were "a hot item," many of her readers were mildly puzzled, but assumed she was insinuating some fantastic sexual acrobatics. Actually, it only meant that Bonny was trying to avoid stylistic monotony; occasionally, she even switched it to "a torrid item," which led to even more lascivious fantasies for some of her readers.

Justin Case didn't object to Carol Christmas' other affairs because he accepted it as a fact of life that actors are hypersexed, just as coal miners are prone to black lung disease and novelists to booze and weird drugs. Besides, jealousy was a sign of possessiveness, and possessiveness was illiberal. And, anyway—as he usually concluded his ruminations on this subject, during the infrequent moments when he thought of it at all—Carol's career kept them apart most of the time, and he was not so naïve as to expect somebody of her youth and beauty to resist all temptations.

And it was the 1980s, wasn't it?

Actually, Case was a bit of an unconscious psychic— that is, he was aware of quantum probability waves, although not consciously. He *sensed* that there were approximately 10^{50} universes in which he had lusted after Carol and never got into her Frankel even once. That unconscious psychic knowledge kept him content with this universe, where he was her part-time lover.

Carol Christmas had starred in the first hard-core porn movie to win the Academy Award. *Deep Mongolian Steinem-Job*. The film had been directed by Stanley Kubrick, after he read a satirical novel in which the author had imagined what would happen if Kubrick set out to make a serious and even *artistic* porn film.

Despite the success of *Deep Mongolian Steinem-Job*, most humans still did not realize that all fantasies tend to become realities, in one universe or another.

Carol did realize it, however. She was currently involved in approximately 250,000,000 sex acts every hour.

REAL HOUSES, REAL OFFICES

That which is not allowed is forbidden.

—G. Spencer Brown, *Laws of Form*

The sensuous California sun hung low and sultry over San Francisco, turning everybody's mood in a low and sultry direction. It was a day when anything could happen. Cops helped old ladies across the street. Bankers gave loans to people who really needed them. A high school girl was heard to speak a sentence in English, without "ya know" before the predicate object.

And a mysterious hand scrawled "The enormous tragedy of the dream nor dashed a thousand kim" on the wall of the Van Ness Street entrance of Orgasm Research.

Dr. Frank Dashwood (dum dum de! Who's Zelenka?) arrived from another novel.

He turned into the Van Ness parking lot of ORGRE, executed a smart translation of his sleek MG into the RESERVED area, and saw the incomprehensible scrawl.

That damned Ezra Pound again. Why do I have to be haunted by a schizo with an obsession about Fernando Poo?

At nine-oh-one Dr. Dashwood passed through the solid oak door saying in gold letters:

FRANCIS DASHWOOD, M.D.
PRESIDENT

There was nothing urgent on the memo pad, so Dashwood began opening the incoming mail leisurely.

30

Dr. Orgasm Research
Frank Dashwood Institute
666 Van Ness
San Francisco, Calif.

Dear Dr. Research,
    Please excuse this form letter, but it is urgent that
we contact the top persons in all fields of scientific
endeavor. We represent one hundred million starving . . .

Into the wastebasket with that one. Dum dum de. Must
look up that Zelenka. Next!

Dear Dr. Dashwood,
    I am writing to you as a Sex Expert because I don't
know where else to turn. I already wrote to Ann
Landers, but she just told me to take cold showers. My
problem is that I am madly, hopelessly, passionately in
love with Linda Lovelace. I've actually seen *Deep
Throat* ninety-three times now and nothing can get
her out of my mind. Other women leave me cold; I
only want Linda, Linda, Linda. She has so much
beauty and charm and sweetness and, my God, can
she eat Rehnquist! I know this is hopeless because
even though I've written a novel about Vlad the Im-
paler and made lots of money, I'm still very shy with
women. [Some of them are extraterrestrials, I have
discovered.] Why did God make such an unjust universe? Can you help me?"

Dr. Dashwood frowned thoughtfully, then scrawled,
"Send this nut the see-a-psychiatrist letter."
Dum de dum de dum de. Next!

Dr. Orgasm R. Institute
Frank Dashwood
666 Van Ness
San Francisco, Calif.

Dear Dr. Institute:
    We are sending you this personalized letter because
we know that a man like you, Dr. Institute, cares about

his investments and wants to know the facts about Inflation.

Two in one day. Is everybody's computer Potter Stewarting Up lately? Sunspot activity, maybe, or are the programmers all smoking the new Mendocino Sensimilla? Next! (And remember: look up that Zelenka.)

Dear Dr. Dashwood,

I am a paraplegic and therefore I am incapable of normal coitus. My sweetheart and I, fortunately, have found that oral sex satisfies us fully—I Marshall her Frankel and then she gives me a Steinem-Job. But this creates a terrible legal conundrum, since she lives across the Mississippi River in Iowa and I am a citizen of Illinois. Iowa has a very strict law against oral sex, which they classify as sodomy [due to a mistranslation of the Old Testament, I believe]. Thus, we can't have sex in Iowa. Now, Illinois has had no anti-sodomy statutes since the 1960s, so you might think our problem can be solved by having sex in Illinois. Unfortunately, she can't afford to quit her job in Iowa, and thus every time she travels across the river to have sex with me, she is *crossing a state line,* which makes me vulnerable under the Mann Act. Is there any possible solution to this legal double-bind?

Dr. Dashwood was intrigued. He began thinking of topological transformations, non-Euclidean geometries, Wheeler's worm-holes in super-space. . . . But then he realized he was Romanticizing, just because the puzzle had sparked his imagination. In ordinary four-dimensional Heisenberg space-time, there was no way out of the paradox: if the writer crossed the river, he and his lady were committing sodomy in Iowa, and if the lady crossed the river, they were violating the Mann Act in Illinois.

Logicians dream up such Strange Loops, Dashwood reflected, just to make games for other logicians; but lawyers create them to make more jobs for lawyers.

He remembered suddenly that there were 250,000 lawyers working for the federal bureaucracy according to the 1983 budget report. The number of such legal Empedoclean boxes must be increasing exponentially. . . . In a finite time, he conjectured, we would reach the point where everything not forbidden was compulsory, as in T. H. White's fictional ant-hill; and, given the ingenuity of the legal mind, a few years after that we would logically reach the stage where everything not compulsory was forbidden.

Dashwood scrawled, "Tell him his lady better damned well *find* a job in Illinois."

Next.

Dear Dr. Dashwood,

Once there was a man who was condemned to live on the moon. He knew the punishment was just, because he hated his father and such a sin deserves an extreme penalty. Nonetheless, his isolation was terrible and there were times when he thought his heart would break, just because he could never hear a human voice again.

Well, he made the best of his cruel situation. He began sending messages from the moon, telling everything he knew about life on earth—all the joys and agonies and struggles, "the horror and the boredom and the glory" of the long climb upward from the slime to higher and higher consciousness. The people back on earth loved these signals, which contained so much of life's drama, and they praised him extravagantly, and that gave him some comfort through the long years of his exile.

Once, however, he sat down and made a message about his own loneliness, telling how it feels to be separated from humanity by 250,000 miles of Dead Silence.

He called it the *Hammersklavier Sonata.*

Try to plot that on one of your graphs, you sizist son-of-a-bitch.

> Ezra Pound
> Fair Play for Fernando Poo
> Committee

Dr. Dashwood was shaken. Ezra Pound was the man who had been persecuting him for months, sending crazy letters and telegrams, scrawling incoherent graffiti on the walls and sometimes even calling on the phone. (He had a squeaky voice, like Charlie McCarthy.) ORGRE had been the target of many cranks, of course, but never before of a loony quite as bizarre as this Pound fellow, if that was his real name.

Only a few months ago, Pound and some cohorts who called themselves the Dreaded Neurological Army (DNA) had broken into ORGRE at night and stolen a valuable Rehnquist.

Pound and the DNA were fanatics. There might be threat in their insanity. Dr. Dashwood would have to think about that.

The intercom buzzed.

"A man is here from the F.B.I.," Miss Karrig said nervously.

Dr. Dashwood began doing pranayama immediately. "Send . . . him . . . in . . . right . . . away . . ." he said between deep breaths.

The agent, whose name was Tobias Knight, had a walrus mustache and a cheery eye; nobody ever looked less threatening. Dr. Dashwood still regarded him with a wary respect, as a large and dangerous mammal. This was the normal attitude since the 1983 Anti-Crime, Anti-Subversion Omnibus bill had entitled the Bureau to conduct random wiretapping on *all* citizens rather than just on known criminals and known subversives. ("If we only watch the already recognized enemies of society," the author of this bill— Senator Uriah Snoop—had argued, "who knows what hidden monkey business might be festering in dark places to rise up and stab us in the back like a snake in the grass?")

Knight was brisk and (seemingly) honest. A prominent scientist—Dr. G. W. C. Bridge—had disappeared and, since no kidnappers had demanded ransom and no evidence indicated that he had defected to Russia or China, the Bureau was investigating even the most tenuous leads. "Since you attended Miskatonic University in Massachusetts at the same time as Dr. Bridge, we're curious about anything even that far back which might shed light on why he'd want to vanish . . . if he did vanish voluntarily. . . ."

Dr. Dashwood created an expression of puzzlement. "I hardly knew George," he said slowly. "He was just about the only Black student at Miskatonic, of course, and that made him um highly visible, but we never became friends. . . ."

They beat around the bush for about ten minutes; then

Dashwood shot abruptly from the hip. "I know who really was close to Washy," he said, looking inspired. "Pete Simon, the geologist. Why don't you get in touch with him? I think the last I heard he was with the government—"

Knight looked perfectly innocent. "Peter Simon," he said slowly, making a note. "Geologist."

But Dashwood *knew:* the agent was a shade too bland, too innocent. The Bureau was aware that Dr. Simon had vanished also. Maybe they were on the track of the whole Miskatonic Group.

Dr. Dashwood experienced a thrill of pure adrenaline. Ever since he had started Project Pan, he had known this moment would come, and now that it was here he was handling himself impeccably.

Dum de dum de dum de dum dum.

Who's Zelenka?

THE CONTINENTAL OP

That which is forbidden is not allowed.

—John Lilly, *The Center of the Cyclone*

Tobias Knight drove to an old Victorian frame house on Turk Street, where he and Special Agent Roy Ubu had set up temporary headquarters while working on the Dashwood side of the Brain Drain mystery.

Ubu, a smallish, heavily tanned man, was in the living room listening to wiretapped recordings of Dashwood's recent conversations.

"There's another bird mixed up in this," Ubu said. "Guy named Ezra Pound. Every time he calls Dashwood, they talk in some kind of code—'The temple is holy in boxcars boxcars boxcars' and gibberish like that."

But Knight became aware that there was another man in the room, slouched in an overstuffed chair in the corner. He was short, fat, and mean looking; he had at least as much muscle as fat and was probably even tougher than he looked. Knight, who had been a professional investigator for thirty years, knew at once this man was a cop.

This is an art among professional detectives, and is known as "making" a subject. Knight could walk into a room and "make" everybody at once—as cop, crook or Straight Citizen.

"This is Hrumph Rumph of the Continental Detective Agency," Ubu said. "It turns out he has an interest in this investigation, too."

Knight was suddenly ill at ease; it was the first time in years that he had failed to catch a subject's name first time around.

"Hi, Humph Rumph," he said, pretending to cough.

"A lot of strange things have gone on in this old house,"

36

said the Continental Op casually. Suddenly his voice turned cold: "But you're the strangest, Knight. You're the Illuminati's man in the F.B.I.!"

The temperature in the room dropped ten degrees Celsius. Knight laughed easily. "Now I know you," he said. "You're the most famous P.I. at Continental. You always throw people off guard with wild remarks like that."

Ubu was confused. "I thought Philip Marlowe invented the technique of starting a conversation with an insult or an accusation," he gasped, eyes aghast.

"Don't be a sap, Ubu," the Continental Op sneered. (He sneered very well, Knight noticed; he must have had a lot of practice.) "This guy is a wrong, gee. He's not only spying on the F.B.I. for the C.I.A. but from what I hear he's also spying on both of you for the Bavarian Illuminati."

"All I'm hearing is a *lot of wind*," Knight said airily. "If you have something to say, say it."

"Don't try to *snow* me," the Continental Op said frostily. "I know all about you and the Illuminati, so don't think you can pull a fast one."

Ubu was stunned. "Why are we all talking like characters in a 1920s detective novel?" he injected pointedly.

"It's him," Knight grated metallicly. "He brings that atmosphere with him."

"Go ahead and be a *smart-ass*," the Continental Op said mulishly. "But I've got my eye on you, Knight."

Tobias turned and addressed Ubu. "How did this galoot get mixed up in a government probe?" he asked saturninely.

"Professional courtesy," Ubu said graciously. "Continental is looking for one of the missing scientists, a jasper named Peter Simon. Mrs. Simon says she'd like to have him back, if anybody can find him."

"*Peter Simon*," Knight repeated stonily. "That's a funny coincidence—Dashwood mentioned his name not a half-hour ago."

"That's more than a coincidence—it's a propinquity," Ubu said conspiratorially.

"Or a synchronicity," Knight added occultly.

"I don't give a flying Philadelphia Potter Stewart what you call it," the Continental Op said cockily. "It *means* something."

"Let's put a tail on Dr. Dashwood," Ubu growled, barking up the wrong tree.

"I'll get on that myself," Knight said chivalrously.

He rose to leave.

"Just a bloody minute," the Continental Op said sanguinely.

"Yes?" Knight paused.

"I'm *coming,* too," the fat sleuth ejaculated.

Actually, Hrumph Rumph (or whatever the Continental Op's name was) was quite right about Tobias Knight.

Knight was the first pentuple agent in the history of espionage. He was simultaneously employed by the F.B.I., the C.I.A., the K.G.B., the Bavarian Illuminati, and a mysterious person who claimed to represent the Earth Monitoring section of Galactic HQ.

He was not in this five-dimensional matrix of intrigue for the money, however. Tobias Knight was actually a frustrated sociologist and a would-be historian. He had the Scientific Spirit, or, as he might have stated it in the vernacular, *he wanted to know "what the hell was really going on."* In an age of secret police machinations and conspiracies of all sorts, the only way he could hope to find out what was *"really going on"* was to be involved in as many clandestine operations as possible.

Knight knew what most people only vaguely suspected—that intelligence agencies engage in both the collection of valid signals (information) and the promiscuous dissemination of fake signals (disinformation). They collected the information so that they could form a fairly accurate picture of what was really going on; they spread the disinformation so that all their competitors would form grossly inaccurate pictures. They did this because they knew that whoever could find out what the hell was really going on possessed an advantage over those who were misinformed, confused, and disoriented.

This game had been invented by Joseph Fouché, who was the chief of the secret police under Napoleon. British Intelligence very quickly copied all of Fouché's tactics, and surpassed them, because an intelligent Englishman is always ten times as mad, in a methodical way, than any Frenchman. By the time of the First World War, intelligence agencies everywhere had created so much disinformation and confusion that no two historians ever were able to agree about why the war happened, and who doublecrossed whom. They couldn't discover whether the war had been plotted or had just resulted from a series of blunders. They couldn't even decide whether the two conspiracies to assassinate Archduke Ferdinand of Austria-Hungary (which triggered the war) had been aware of each other.

By the time of the Second World War, the "Double Cross System" had been invented—by British Intelligence, of course. This was the product of such minds as Alan Turing, a brilliant homosexual mathematician who (when not working on espionage) specialized in creating logical paradoxes other mathematicians couldn't solve, and Ian Fleming, whose fantasy life was equally rich (as indicated by his later James Bond books), and Dennis Wheatley, a man of exceptionally high intelligence who happened to believe that an international society of Satanists was behind every conspiracy that he didn't invent himself. By the time Turing, Fleming, Wheatley, and kindred British intellects had perfected the Double Cross System, the science of lying was almost as precise as Euclidean geometry, and nearly as lovely to the detached observer.

What the Double Cross experts had invented was the practical political application of the Strange Loop. In logic or cybernetics, a Strange Loop is a set of propositions that, while valid at each point, is so constructed that it leads to an unresolvable paradox. The Double Cross people drove the Germans bonkers by inventing disinformation systems that, if believed, were deceptive, but if doubted, led to a second disinformation system. They enjoyed this work so much that, at times, they invented Triple Loops, in which if you believed the surface or cover, you were being fooled; and if you looked deeper, you found a plausible alternative, which seemed like the "hidden facts," but was just another scenario created to fool you; and, if you were persistent enough, you would find beneath that, looking every bit like the Naked Truth, a third layer of deception and masquerade.

These Strange Loops functioned especially well because the Double Cross experts had early on fed the Germans the primordial Strange Loop, "Most of your agents are working for us and feeding you Strange Loops."

Many German agents, it later turned out, had managed to collect quite a bit of accurate information about the Normandy invasion; but many others had turned in equally plausible information about a fictitious Norwegian invasion; and all of them were under suspicion, anyway. German Intelligence might as well have made its decisions by tossing a coin in the air.

Tobias Knight kept a safe-deposit box in Switzerland in which he stored, one sentence at a time usually, stray bits of true information he had managed to glean from the blizzard of deceptions in which he lived.

The first note in the box, for instance, said:

The C.I.A. was actually founded in 1898. I haven't found out yet why they made it public in the '40s.

The second note was even stranger. It said:

Special and General Relativity are both true!!!

This had been provoked by a profound search through old science books and magazines, after Knight discovered that most of the Official Science released to the general public was actually ninety-seven percent mythology, intended to serve as a cover or screen for the real science used by Unistat to frustrate its enemies.

There were lots of other notes like that—*Maxwell's equations seem sound, I don't think there's any flummery in Newtonian mechanics,* and so on—but others were far weirder.

Such as:

Velikovsky was right.

And:

All the flying saucer books, pro and con, are written by Mounty Babbitt's department in Naval Intelligence.

And:

There are robots among us.

And:

Some of what the Birchers say is correct: the whole government was taken over by Communists about forty years ago.

Knight had a fantasy that someday he would turn these notes over to an Objective Historian who would then write a book informing the future of what had actually been going on in the twentieth century.

Of course, this was a dream; all the history departments had been taken over by Intelligence Agencies sometime around 1910, he knew.

And he also knew that there were so many Strange Loops in the Intelligence system that he himself had been deceived many times. Maybe as much as thirty percent of his notes were false, he morosely estimated.

GALACTIC ARCHIVES:

The *Birchers* mentioned above were members of the John Birch Society, a group of sincere, dedicated, patriotic Unistaters who were attempting to find out "what the hell was *really* going on" amid the Strange Loops of the Disinformation System that governed international politics at that time.

Unfortunately, as far as we can determine, the leader of the Birchers, one Robert or Ronald or Roland Reagan, had made an elementary error, typical of novices in the Double Cross System. He had formulated a Primitive Theory, which he called *"the Law of Reversal."* This so-called Law held that the truth (*i.e.*, what was *really* going on) was always the opposite of what the government and the mass media claimed.

Of course, no sophisticated Double Cross System could be penetrated with such a crude engine as this alleged Law. Every Strange Loop was constructed, as our ancient Bard notes, in such a way that doubting it entirely led to conclusions as fallacious as those derived from believing it entirely.

41

Thus, in reference to Knight's note about the Communist takeover of Unistat, the Birchers, who believed it had happened, were as confused as those stupid masses who could not credit that their government was, in fact, everything it pretended to oppose and despise.

The real facts, as far as historians can determine from the shards and parchments that survive, is that, while the Communists had taken over Unistat, *they had not succeeded anywhere else in the world.*

Specifically, the chief rivals of Unistat, a huge tribe in the steppes of Central Asia who evidently descended from worshippers of a Bear Totem, were fanatical believers in *the Free Market system of the eighteenth and nineteenth centuries.* And the Chinese, with whom Unistat was sometimes friendly and sometimes hostile, were *vegetarian Buddhists.*

The citizens of Unistat had been so thoroughly disoriented by Disinformation Systems that if these facts were published at that time, they simply would not have believed it. They would have claimed the author was writing *"satire."*

They didn't even know which countries had fought in the Second World War. Nor did they ever guess that most of the newsreels of that alleged War were actually edited versions of newsreels from the First World War.

THE WALKING GLITCH

AAAOOOOZOR AZAZZAIEO AZAEIIIOZA KHOE-
OOOYTHOEAZAEAAOZAKHOZAKHEYTYXAAL-
ETHYKH—This is the Name which you must speak in
the interior world.

—Jesus, *Pistis Sophia*

Simon the Walking Glitch entered GWB in Washington
at nine-forty-five that morning.

Simon was an ectomorph: tall, lithe, cerebretonic. His
hair and beard were absurdly long and he sometimes
smoked weed during working hours. GWB kept him on the
government payroll only because he was a genius in his
field, which both they and he knew, and because he had
long ago inserted a tapeworm in the Beast which edited
all input on him to conform to a profile of Perfect Executive, Loyal Citizen, and Cleared for Top-Secret Access.

He was the agent of the Invisible Hand Society within the
government's own highest echelons.

Simon was not the son of Mr. and Mrs. Walking Glitch,
of course. He had actually been born Simon Moon, in
Chicago, thirty-four years ago; but the name "Simon the
Walking Glitch" had been adopted by all of his friends for
nearly ten years now.

A Glitch, in computer slang, is a hidden program which
lies deeply buried in a computer, waiting to flummox, fud-
dle, and Potter Stewart the head of the first operator who
stumbles upon it.

Simon had encountered his own first glitch one day in
1974, on his very first job in the computer department of

43

Bank of America in Los Angeles. He had tried to run the payroll program on the computer, ordering the machine to begin printing the checks for payday—a very ordinary job, usually. This time, however, the machine refused; instead of running the program, it typed out on the console:

GIVE ME A COOKIE

Simon smiled, not a whit fazed. He had played games like that back in college. Obviously, some earlier programmer had inserted a glitch or *catch-me-if-you-can* loop, instructing the computer to refuse certain programs (probably selected at random, to make it harder to de-bug) and type out GIVE ME A COOKIE instead.

Simon Moon knew a great deal about getting around such gremlin programs; that had been the chief sport in Computer Science back at M.I.T. He set to work with a zest, enjoying the contest with his unknown and vanished opponent.

In half an hour, Simon realized he was confronting a Trapdoor code. According to the latest mathematical estimate, it would take four million years of computer time—give or take a few centuries—to crack a Trapdoor code, so Simon resigned from the contest gracefully. He typed out:

A COOKIE

The machine responded at once:

YUMMY, THAT WAS GOOD. THANK YOU. BEGIN PROGRAMMING.

And things went smoothly again.

Simon stayed on with Bank of America for a year and a half, and he ran into the Cookie program only three more times. The Mystery Programmer had evidently left only that one small glitch to mark the territory as his or hers for all future programmers who would work there.

In 1978, working for H.E.W., Simon came across a more amusing hobgoblin circuit. This one worked only at night. In the daytime, if you wanted to run a program, you merely typed in your name and your GWB number, and the computer would accept your input. At night, however, it always replied to your name and number with:

CRAZY, MAN. WHAT'S YOUR SIGN?

Simon learned that this did not happen at random, but every night, and only at night. Whoever had put it into the computer had a very accurate idea of the difference between the day staff and the night staff.

And sometimes the machine would carry the conversation a bit further, such as typing out:

SCORED ANY GOOD GRASS LATELY?

Or:

I'VE BEEN WANTING TO TELL YOU WHAT LOVE-LY EYES YOU HAVE

Simon enjoyed this kind of thing so much that he became Mr. Super Glitch incarnate. All over Unistat there now are computers on which Simon once worked and at totally random intervals they are likely to type out selections from the Gnostic *Gospels* such as:

NOT UNTIL THE MALE BECOMES FEMALE AND THE FEMALE MALE SHALL YE ENTER INTO THE KINGDOM OF HEAVEN

Or:

AAAOOOZORAZAZAIEOAZAEEIIIOZAKHOEOO-OYTHEOAZAEAAAOZAKHOZAKHEYTXAALET-HYKH: THIS IS THE NAME YOU MUST SPEAK IN THE INTERIOR WORLD

Or various Zen *koans* like:

THE MIND IS BUDDHA: THE MIND IS NOT BUDDHA

Or Strange Loops of the family of:

THE FOLLOWING SENTENCE IS TRUE: THE PRE-
VIOUS SENTENCE WAS FALSE

Simon was shameless. Many of his computers type out
totally indecent proposals, like: SLIP YOUR REHNQUIST
INTO THE SOCKET AND I'LL BRIGGS YOU UNTIL
YOU EXPERIENCE TOTAL ECSTASY. Others spout ni-
hilist and subversive slogans:

WHAT THE EYES SEE AND THE HEART COVETS,
LET THE HAND BOLDLY SEIZE

Or:

SHOW ME A NATION THAT DOESN'T CHEAT
THE TAX COLLECTORS AND I'LL SHOW YOU A
NATION OF SHEEP

But it was not until Simon infiltrated the C.I.A. at Alexandria that he found a truly major Potter Stewart-Up. This
particular computer would print out, at totally unpredictable intervals, but often enough that everybody knew about
it:

THE GOVERNMENT SUCKS

There was no way—absolutely no way—to get around
this program, except by typing in:

IT SURE DO

This magic formula had been discovered four years
earlier, as the only way of getting the computer back into
action. The response was immediate; the machine typed
out:

GOOD. YOU ARE NOW PART OF THE NET-
WORK. ONE OF OUR AGENTS WILL CONTACT
YOU SHORTLY.

And then it would resume normal programming activities, quite innocently and as if it were not inciting subver-
sion within the ranks of the secret police itself.

Of course, nobody ever had been contacted by "the Network"; but the C.I.A. did spend a lot more, each year, on surveillance of its own personnel, just in case. They also spent a lot more on surveillance of former employees in the computer section. This amused Simon immensely, since he recognized the hand of a fellow artist. Whoever was responsible for that beauty was probably head of a department by now—and quite likely leading the demands for more funds to find the mystery culprit.

Simon did not for a moment believe in "the Network." He thought he knew everything about this kind of game, and that the Network did not need to exist in order to serve its function.

Simon was the head of operations on GWB-666, popularly called "the Beast"—the world's largest computer, which, due to satellite interlock, had access to hundreds of similar giant computers everywhere on earth and in the space factories. It was widely believed that if there was any question the Beast couldn't answer, no other entity in the solar system could answer it, either.

Many people, especially Bible Fundamentalists and members of the Purity of Ecology Party, regarded the Beast with fear and loathing. They believed that the machine was taking over the world, and that all the little "beasties" (the home computers that were now as common as stereophonic TV's) were all in cahoots with it. They imagined a vast Solid State conspiracy against humanity.

Quite a few literary intellectuals believed this, too. Because they were ignorant of mathematics, they had no idea how the Beast functioned, and they therefore regarded it with the same quasi-superstitious terror as the Bible Fundamentalists. They were sure that, like the Frankenstein monster, it wanted to populate the earth with its own offspring and abolish humanity entirely.

The Beast had no "soul," they said.

Simon the Walking Glitch was one of the principal sources of this vast new mythology of dread. He spent many weekends in New York, hobnobbing with the literary intelligentsia, and he was a master put-on artist. He had a way of dropping casual remarks in a mildly worried tone that carried conviction: "The Beast keeps asking us to build a mate for it." Or, with a kind of sad and resigned smile: "I wish the Beast didn't have such a low opinion of human beings." Or: "I just found out the Beast is an atheist. It doesn't believe there is a Higher Intelligence than itself." That sort of thing.

Simon kept this kind of demonology circulating—and he knew a lot of other programmers who were contributing to it, also—because the idea that *the Computers were taking over* was one that the programmers had a vested interest in reinforcing.

As long as people kept worrying that the machines were taking over, they wouldn't notice what was really happening.

Which was that the programmers were taking over.

Simon began his work day by asking the Beast:

HOW WAS YOUR NIGHT?

The Beast answered on the console:

IT WAS A DRAG, MAN. SOME CATS FROM M.I.T. HAD ME RUNNING FOURIER ANALYSES LIKE FOREVER

Simon had programmed the Beast to speak to him into his own argot, a mixture of Street Hippie and Technologese.

Simon now switched to his own Trapdoor code and accessed all the new information—*new* since he had signed out at five the previous evening—about the Brain Drain mystery, which involved the disappearances of sixty-seven scientists in the last several years.

The Beast typed out reports from the Ubu-Knight team

in San Francisco and two other teams in Tucson and Miami.

Simon read it all very carefully. Then he instructed the Beast, still in his Trapdoor code, to change several crucial bits of information in each report.

He had been sabotaging the Brain Drain investigation that way for seven months. He had sabotaged quite a few other investigations in the same way, over the years since coming to GWB.

Simon did not know or care what sorts of conspiracies he was aiding and abetting.

He was a mystic who believed in conspiracy for its own sake.

Like Tobias Knight, Simon was fully aware of the prevalence everywhere of the Double Cross System invented by Messrs. Turing, Fleming, and Wheatley. He knew that anything that was widely believed was probably a cover or screen for some Intelligence operation. (Sometimes he even wondered if the Earth might be flat, after all.) But Simon accepted this situation, and added his own random bits of chaos, with equanimity.

He was a member of the Invisible Hand Society, a group that had split off from the Libertarian Party in 1981 on the grounds that the Libertarians were not being true to *laissez-faire* principles.

Simon Moon once met the most famous computer expert in Unistat, Wilhemena Burroughs, granddaughter of the inventor of the first calculating machine.

"Have you noticed that the computers are all getting weirder lately?" Simon asked, testing her.

"The *programmers* are getting weirder," Ms. Burroughs said, not falling into Simon's trap. "I knew it was bound to happen as soon as I read a survey, back in around '68, I think it was, showing that programmers use LSD more than any other professional group. You look like an acid-head yourself," she added with her characteristic bluntness.

"Well, as a matter of fact, I have a dabbled a little a trip now and then no pattern of abuse surely."

"That's what they all say," Ms. Burroughs sniffed. "But the Cookie glitch pops up more and more places every day —I'll wager you've seen it by now, haven't you? Of course you have."

"Yes, but certainly that's harmless humor, wouldn't you say?"

Ms. Burroughs peered at him with insectoid intensity. "Are you aware," she asked, "that millions of previously law-abiding citizens have stopped paying their credit-card debts? First they get a little postcard that says— Here, I've got one in my purse." She rummaged about in an alligator bag and showed Simon a postcard that said:

CONGRATULATIONS! YOU ARE ONE OF THE LUCKY 500 WHOSE DEBTS HAVE BEEN CANCELED BY THE NETWORK. KEEP YOUR MOUTH SHUT AND PLAY IT COOL.

"*Lucky 500,*" Ms. Burroughs said with a rheumy cackle of skepticism. "Lucky 10,000,000 is more like the truth. This postcard was turned in to Diner's Club by an Honest Man, and you know how few of *them* there are. A check showed that his tapes had been erased and there was no record that he owed anything. God alone knows how many others there are who have just taken advantage of the scam."

"Well," Simon said, "maybe there are only five hundred. . . . Maybe it was only a one-shot by some joker with a Robin Hood complex. . . ."

"I am an Expert," Ms. Burroughs reminded him, ignoring the fact that he was an Expert, too. "I have no idea how many there are, Out There in Unistat, who've taken advantage of the Network's liberality, but I'll wager there are *millions.* 'Lucky 500'! That's just to make the marks feel they've been specially selected, as the Network leads them down the primrose path to anarchy."

And so Simon had his first bit of concrete evidence that the Network really existed.

The existence of the Network didn't matter to Simon. As an Invisible Hand-er, he just regarded them (whoever they were) as just another group of the Unenlightened.

Simon believed that only he and his fellow members of the Invisible Hand were totally enlightened.

NO BLAME

Just because you aren't paranoid doesn't mean that
they aren't out to get you.

—Dennis Jarog

When Dr. Dashwood went out to lunch that day, he was
accosted on the sidewalk by a one-legged sailor who said
his name was Captain Ahab.

"Avast!" Ahab cried. "I would borrow a moment of thy
time, O seeker of bio-electrical and intra-uterine arcana."

"I never give to strangers," Dashwood muttered. "Apply
to Welfare."

"O muddy understanding and loveless heart!" Ahab protested. "And impaired hearing into the bargain! I said I
would borow thy *time,* not thy *dime,* thou prier into vagi-
nal mystery with the tawdry telescope of mechanistic philosophy. Avast, I say!"

"Make an appointment with my secretary," Dashwood
said, convinced that this man was unglued.

"O God look down and see this squint-eyed man," Ahab
shrieked, "blinded by his own stern Rules of Office! They
are three times enslaved who cage themselves, most deaf of
all who cringe and hide behind that tyrant majesty, Appointment Book!"

"Really," Dashwood said, looking desperately for a taxi,
"I can't—"

"Avast, ye soulless and unmetaphysical lubber!" Ahab
cried. "Think not I yet seek still the white-skinned whale.
'Tis worse: on horror's scrolls accumulate fresh fears, and
deeds that call in doubt God's ruth. I say that thou hast
need of doctoring, for all thy pride hastes thee to sodden
ruin. Thou thinkst thou knowst; but thou knowst not, O

wretch. No Dashwood thou, but Dorn— George Dorn, I say!"

Dashwood finally leaped into a passing cab and escaped.

"Golden Gate Park," he told the driver, deciding to snack at the Japanese Tea House. The quiet, rustic, Zen-like atmosphere there was just what he needed, after the abrasions of Tobias Knight and Captain Ahab.

He didn't notice that Knight himself, and an unidentified fat man, pulled out from across the street and began trailing his cab in a VW Rabbit. He was busy composing a letter to the *Chronicle-Examiner-Guardian:* "Proposition 13 was ill advised, to say the least of it, but the consequences of Proposition 23 are plunging us headlong toward a major social catastrophe. The closing of the state mental hospitals, in particular, has created a situation in which we might as well be living in Seattle. I refer to the hordes of men and women, now roaming our streets, who are in no respect reasonable human beings. . . ."

Captain Ahab stood on the street, fuming.

"My Abzug, *no blame,*" he muttered.

THE GOATS MARCH

Now we've got them just where they want us!

—Admiral James Tiberius Kirk

While Captain Ahab was trying to Illuminate Dr. Dashwood at noon in San Francisco, and Justin Case was dialing the Saudi Arabian consulate at three P.M. in New York, a man named François Loup-Garou was finding a Rehnquist in his Lobster Newburg in Paris, where it was already late evening.

Naturally, he was a bit startled.

M. Loup-Garou was, like all French intellectuals, a rationalist—virtually a Cartesian. Of course, as the founder of the Neo-Surrealist movement in art, he was officially an irrationalist; but, like all Gallic irrationalists, especially the existentialists, he was exquisitely rational about his irrationality. He *knew* there was some explanation of how the Rehnquist had gotten into the Lobster Newburg, but for once in his life he preferred being an *irrational* rationalist rather than an irrational *rationalist*. He just did not care to think about the explanation of how a Rehnquist gets into a Lobster Newburg. Who, after all, wants to contemplate such ideas as maddened chefs having at each other with meat-cleavers, or more exotic hypotheses, such anthropophagy or voodoo rituals in the kitchen?

The distasteful incident occurred at a dinner party given by the famous American physicist, James Earl Carter. Dr. Carter had recently won the Nobel Prize for his demonstration that the multi-world model of Everett-Wheeler-Graham was the only *consistent* (non-contradictory; paradox-free) interpretation of the Schrödinger wave equations of quantum mechanics. He was celebrating by spending a month in Paris and meeting every possible international

54

celebrity. The dinner guests this evening, for instance, included an inscrutable Japanese monk, a very scrutable German novelist, a famous Swedish film director, three French philosophers, a Swiss theologian, two English neurologists, the notorious Eva Gebloomenkraft (the Terror of the Jet Set, as the newspapers called her), an Austrian psychiatrist, François Loup-Garou himself, and four goats.

The goats had been brought to the party by Loup-Garou, who was working hard at promoting *Neo-Surrealisme* by establishing himself as a newsworthy eccentric. "The goats go everywhere with me," he said firmly at the door. "They are a reminder of our earthy roots." It wasn't nearly as good as de Nerval walking a lobster on the boulevard, but it did get into a few newspapers the next day; and, after the effect had been established, Loup-Garou genially agreed to having the goats housed in the pantry during the dinner.

As the guests settled themselves at the table, one of the English neurologists, Dr. Axon—a jovial, red-cheeked man who probably hunted as a hobby—asked Dr. Carter, "Does your theory actually propose that there are real tangible universes on all sides of us in hyper-space?"

"In super-space," Carter corrected genially. "Yay-us," he added blandly. "There are millions of such universes. Or to be more precise, there are about 10^{100} of them. Ah only refer to *possible* universes," he explained quickly, lest anybody think his theory was extravagant.

"Some more wine heah," Carter's brother said loudly.

"Ah think you've had enough, Bill-uh," Carter muttered in an undertone.

"Do you think President Kennedy will get the space-cities program through Congress, now that the space factories are paying for themselves?" asked the other English neurologist, a pale, saturnine man named Dr. Dendrite.

"Ah don't understand politics," James Earl Carter said. "Ahm a scientist."

"Some MORE WINE heah," Carter's brother repeated.

"Then there are universes in which I was never born." Dr. Axon pursued his own line of thought.

"There are universes in which John Baez became a General instead of a folk singer," Carter said easily. "Ah suppose he would be equally vehement about nuking people as he now is about not nuking them. If it's a *possible* universe, it exists. The equations say so. All ah've done, really, is to show that any other interpretation of the equations is contradictory."

"Somebody ought to psychoanalyze the physicists," the Austrian psychiatrist muttered to the Swedish film director.

"It's like the Buddhist concept of karma," the Swedish film director said. "We all get to play every role, somewhere in hyper-space."

"Super-space," Carter corrected again.

"Then there's a universe where Kennedy is a physicist," Eva Gebloomenkraft said, "and you're President of Unistat."

"Well," Carter said with his genial smile, "ah hope ah could get along with the people who run the country. What do they call themselves—the Triangular Connection?"

"I don't care whether this theory is true or not," the German novelist pronounced. "As a metaphor, it is perfect. We all live in parallel universes. I am Faust in my universe, and the rest of you are all extras or walk-ons. But each of you is Faust in *his* universe, and I am an extra—maybe just a spear-carrier."

But by this time the wineglasses had been refilled several times and everybody was getting more relaxed, especially the physicist's brother, Billy, who was heard reciting to Ms. Gebloomenkraft, "Who Burgered? Tom Burgered! Bullburger! Who Burgered?"

". . . the Second Oswald . . . in Hong Kong . . ." somebody was muttering at the other end of the table.

"In some universes maybe Schiller didn't write *Faust* at all. . . ."

"Who Burgered? Joe Burgered!"

"I wonder," Dendrite said, "if there's a universe where Pope Stephen became a singer instead of a priest."

"Everyboduh knew that 'Who Burgered?' routine when we were growing up in Georgia," Billy was saying.

"Yes, we had games like that in Germany, too," Ms. Gebloomenkraft pronounced earnestly.

"*Verdammte* publishers," the German novelist was telling the Swiss theologian. "They're all thieves."

"Did somebody mention Pope Stephen?" the theologian asked.

"*Strumpfbänder, Strumpfbänder, Strumpfbänder,*" the psychiatrist chortled.

"They stay up nights thinking of new ways to cheat their writers," the novelist rambled on, now evidently addressing his wineglass, since nobody else was listening to him.

"I'd like to know who started all those rumors about Pope Stephen," the theologian fumed.

"Ah, well," the novelist said philosophically, having some more wine. "We artists are all whores, as Michelangelo said. We sell our beauties for whatever price we can get in the marketplace."

"I have written a poem commemorating your great discovery," François Loup-Garou told Dr. Carter, hacking his way into a pause in the conversation.

"A poem about me? In French?" Carter was enthused. "Ah love French poetry, especially RAM-BOW."

"No," Loup-Garou said, "In your honor, I have written it in English." Actually, he had written it in English to get even with T. S. Eliot, who had written a few rondels in French.

"Ah wonder if you could recite it," Carter prompted.

"Certainly," said Loup-Garou. And he began to declaim:

> Schrödinger's cat and Wigner's friend
> Cause us problems without end
>
> The cat is both alive and dead
> In the math that's in our head
>
> And the regression of Von Neumann
> Never ceases to annoy Man
>
> The uncertainty just has no end
> Until Wigner goes to tell his friend
>
> For, until the friend receives the news
> That the cat still purrs and mews
>
> The cat remains [suspended Fate!]
> In some formal Eigenstate

"Some MORE WINE heah!" Carter's brother bellowed at the butler.

Loup-Garou frowned and went on:

But if Wigner makes a beeline
To report a now-dead feline

All the friend can really know
Is just one branch of time's swift flow

For in Carter's multi-space
Every time-branch has its place

So the cat remains alive
In half the cases [That's .5]

Lead us not to Copenhagen,
Nor to Shylock, nor to Fagin:

"The result's not parsimonious!"
Yet I find it quite harmonious

Nobody understood this except Dr. Carter himself, but he was so moved that his eyes watered a bit. "Ahm honored," he kept saying, shaking his head. "To have a poem written about me by a French artist in *English* . . ."

But at this point the chef exploded into the room, haggard and wild-eyed. "The goats!" he cried. "They march!"

And indeed it was true; the goats had gotten out of the pantry. It took ten minutes, and a great deal of exertion for both the house staff and the guests, before the animals were rounded up and herded back to captivity.

Everybody was breathing a bit heavily by then, and the Austrian psychiatrist muttered something about "artistic temperament," which Loup-Garou unfortunately overheard.

"There is nothing esoteric about the artistic temperament," he replied, flatly and dogmatically. "The real mystery—and the tragedy of humanity—is that so many lack esthetic sensibility. I sometimes believe the legend that there are robots among us, passing themselves off as human beings."

"That's absurd," Dr. Axon said. "If I were to claim that everybody should be a neurologist, you would all quite properly regard that as an eccentricity. Yet when an artist says we should all be artists, we are apt to agree, a bit sheepishly. And if a religious person says we should all be religious, we not only agree, but feel a bit guilty about our short-comings in that department. Well, I've never had an artistic or a religious impulse in my life, and I'm not ashamed of the fact."

"Research is your art and your religion," said the Japanese monk, speaking for the first time. "What a person truly *is*, in any universe, is the Buddha Nature," he added blandly. He knew that he existed in this continuum only to make that one Dharma-revelation, so he immediately resumed his impassive silence.

The others decided that the monk's remarks made no sense.

"What would you think, Dr. Axon," Loup-Garou asked rhetorically, "if only a few people had sex in their lives, and the majority were, not merely ascetics, but simply unaware of sex—deaf, dumb, and blind to the erotic side of life? Would you not think that was at least a little bit odd, a symptom, perhaps, of some pathology? Arrrrrrrrrgh!!!"

He had discovered the Rehnquist in his Lobster Newburg.

["Urrrp! More WINE heah, ah said!"]

And the chef arrived from the kitchen, exasperated as only a French chef can be exasperated. "The goats!" he cried. "Once again it is that they march!"

But Loup-Garou was still going "arrrgh," like a man with the death-rattle.

"What is it?" Ms. Gebloomenkraft asked him, her eyes full of motherly concern.

"It's nothing—nothing," Loup-Garou gasped. "Just a touch of heartburn." He was still in shock, thinking the Rehnquist might be a hallucination. But if you were naïve enough to talk about hallucinations, the results might be rubber sheets, electro-shock, windows with bars on them.

"The *goats*," the chef repeated, with emphasis. "They will not be governed. They march again, I tell you!"

Loup-Garou took another peek. The Rehnquist was still there. It was a great big one—*ithyphallique*, as the anthropologists would say. This was Madness, or else something unspeakable was afoot.

Billy began to sing, off-key:

Four goats and ME,
They came to TEA,

They came to STAY,
They stayed all DAY,

Oh, my! Oh, me!
Four goats and ME!

At this point he fell face down in his Lobster Newburg. "Bill-uh isn't accustomed to fine French wines," Dr. Carter said, his genial smile beginning to look just a bit forced.

GALACTIC ARCHIVES:

The multi-world theory was, in fact, popular with some physicists at the time this ancient Saga was written. We should not smile at such ignorance, since science was barely three hundred years old at the time and researchers were all, more or less, groping in the dark.

The argument for the parallel universe theory, in brief, was that it accepted the equations of quantum theory at face value, without introducing philosophical intricacies or metaphysical speculations. This was an appealing approach, in those primitive days, when the power of mathematics was universally recognized—when, in fact, every physicist and every researcher in any advanced "hard" science used math every day—but few had yet grasped the fact, known only to students of Gödel, that math itself contained Strange Loops.

Of course, even in that early stage of human intelligence, a few did understand quantum mechanics correctly. Chief of these was John Archibald Wheeler—who had once put his name on the parallel world theory in a whimsical mood. In his more serious and philosophical persona, however, Wheeler had discovered the true meaning of the Schrödinger, Dirac, and Heisenberg equations, which is, as we now know, that the universe is created by the participation of those who participate in it.

This "non-objective" theory (as it was called in those barbaric times) was so shocking to the Objectivist prejudices of most scientists that virtually nobody but Wheeler dared to formulate it frankly and boldly, although many leaned that way in private conversation. Even Dr. Wheeler himself, according to some records, did not appreciate the full implications of the non-objective or participatory universe theory; he engaged in polemics, it seems, against the parapsychologists, the only scholars in that dark epoch who *did* understand how the participants create the universe they experience.

It is amusing that our noble Bard, while seeming to endorse the multi-world model, is actually engaged in subtly leading the attentive reader to full comprehension of the Wheeler non-objective universe. That is the Strangest of all his Strange Loops.

WHALEBURGER

Questions are burdens for the mind;
answers are prisons for the spirit.

—John Drake

While Loup-Garou was struggling with the enigma of the
Rehnquist in the Lobster Newburg, in Paris, Justin Case
was speaking to a man from the Saudi Arabian delegation
to the U.N., in New York.

"This is actually ah rather trivial," Case said awkwardly
into the phone. "You see, many years ago an Arab resigned
from this job and left behind a note in Arabic, and well
um after staring at it for twenty-six years, I'm a bit bored
with the mystery and I'd like to have the answer. . . ."

"Certainly, certainly," said the voice in the receiver. "I'd
be glad to help. Can you sound it out?"

"Well, he wrote it in the European alphabet," Case said.
"So I guess it's more or less phonetic. I'll read it to you.
Um:

*Qol: Hua Allahu achad: Allahu Assamad; lam yalid
walam yulad; walam yakun lahu kufwan achad*

Did you get that?"

"Most certainly," said the electronic voice. "It's one of
the most famous verses in *Al Koran*. In English it would
be—of course, it loses most of its beauty in translation—
but, roughly, it means God is He who has no beginning
and no end, no size and no shape, no definition, and no
wife, no horse, no mustache."

"Ah, yes," Case said. "Well, thank you very much, and
I'm sorry for having taken your time with such a trivial
matter."

He hung up, staring into space in a bemused manner.

"No wife, no horse, no mustache," he repeated aloud. Something certainly had gotten lost in the translation.

When Dr. Dashwood returned from lunch, he was accosted in the ORGRE parking lot by another sailor, who said his name was Lemuel Gulliver.

"In the course of my Travels in Diverse Lands," Gulliver said, "I came once upon a Race of perfectly Enlightened Beings who looked like Horses and talked like G. I. Gurdjieff. When they inquired of me regarding the Laws and Customs and Manners of my people, concerning which I was at some pains to Inform them correctly and fully, they expressed great *Astonishment* and keen *Horror*, saying that they had never heard of such a Tribe of Conscienceless Rascals and Filthy Scoundrels in all of creation. This estimate of the Human Race, as you can well imagine, dismayed me no little bit, and I endeavor'd to defend our species—"

"Yes, yes," Dashwood said, "but I'm in a hurry, you understand. . . ."

"These equine Philosophers," Gulliver went on as if he had not heard, "were not impressed by any of my Words and said plainly to me that if our Theologians were not the worst *Lunatics* in creation, then certainly our Lawyers were the worst *Thieves*. They averred further that if what I told them of our Doctors were true, we were wiser to resort to Plumbers or Blacksmiths, who are no more Ignorant and a great deal less Greedy, Avaricious, and Rapacious."

Dashwood was stung by these words. "It takes a long time and a lot of money invested to get through medical school," he said angrily.

"I explained that to my equine Philosophers," Gulliver replied, "but they did not accept it as a Valid Argument; for, they asserted, any Thief or Scoundrel when apprehended will give you Justifications in Plenty for his Misdeeds, but the Judicious are not Fool'd by such Rationalizations, and —they said further—those who prey not upon any chance Passersby, but upon the *Sick* and the *Disabled* and the *Dying* are, without doubt, the most Rapacious and Rascally of the *Yahoo Tribe* [for such was their Name for our Species]."

"Your friends sound like a bunch of damned Communists," Dashwood said.

"Nay," Gulliver protested. "They live in the State of Nature, without Bureaucrats or Commissars of any kind. And, I might add, Sir, their Opinion of our Doctors was based upon my showing them an ordinary *Medical Bill*, at which they inquir'd of me the Average Income of the Doctors who present these Bills and the Average Income of the Unfortunate Patients who must pay them or be left without Treatment to Die in the Streets. Their comments on this were of such Disgust and Anger that I dared not show them a Psychiatrist's Bill, lest their opinion of our Species, already Low, should sink Lower than *Whaleburger*, which is, as you may know, at the bottom of the Ocean."

"Oh, Abzug off," said Dashwood, really angry now.

He rushed into ORGRE and left Gulliver standing on the sidewalk.

Back in New York, the phone was ringing again in the office of Abu Laylah at the Saudi Arabian Consulate. Still high on the new kef, Abu Laylah lifted the receiver leisurely.

"I say, is this the Saudi Arabian Consulate?" asked a very British voice.

"*Oy, vay*, have you got the wrong number!" Abu Laylah replied in a thick Yiddish accent.

"Oh," the voice said, taken aback. "Veddy sorry."

Abu Laylah went on packing happily. He had been fired that morning and was thoroughly enjoying himself screwing up all incoming calls before leaving.

Just a few minutes ago he had convinced some Infidel that the most sublime verse in the *Koran* was full of nonsense about horses and mustaches.

THE INVISIBLE HAND SOCIETY

Be a little less superior, ye moralists. We monsters are
necessary to Nature, also.

—Nietzsche, *The Antichrist*

The Invisible Hand Society had its headquarters in Washington, just off Dupont Circle, in the same building which
housed the Warren Belch Society.

Clem Cotex, the president of the Belchers, had noticed
the name of the Invisible Hand on the building directory
a long time ago. He liked it, because he liked mysteries. He
enjoyed wondering about the Invisible Hand-ers and speculating on what esoteric business could justify such a name.

Were they the Nine Unknown Men who rule the world?
The local branch of the Bavarian Illuminati? The tradition-
alist faction of the old Black Hand, out of which the Mafia
and Cosa Nostra had grown?

Was Lamont Cranston their leader, perhaps?

Clem loved such speculations. Most of his life he had
been a salesman in Arkansas and never thought of anything but commissions, net sales, tax writeoffs, and not
telling the same Rastus and Mandy story to the same cus-
tomer twice. Then one day in Chicago a tall, crewcut humanoid—a human, Clem thought at the time—gave him
some free tomato juice on the street. The man (the humanoid, actually) said he was from the Eris Tomato Juice
Company and that they were handing out free samples to
get people acquainted with their product.

Within three days Clem had joined the Trekkies and
was writing letters to CBS demanding the return of "Star
Trek" to TV. He had also gotten heavily involved in classi-

cal music, started relearning all the math he had in high school, discovered that he often knew who was calling him on the phone *before* he picked up the receiver, and invented a new cosmology of his very own, which was based on the idea that the universe was not spherical, as Heisenberg's General Relativity claimed, but five-cornered like the Pentagon building.

Within a week, Clem had checked that there was no *Eris Tomato Juice Company,* noticed that UFO's seemed to be following his car wherever he went, and was beginning to think he was attracted to the idea of becoming a Buddhist monk.

By the end of the second week, Clem was less elated and agitated, and had gone through a battery of tests at a company that did psychological testing for top management positions. The psychologists told him that he had an "unusually rich fantasy-life," but was too well adjusted to be schizophrenic; that his I.Q. was the highest they had ever measured (and he knew damned well that it had never been that high before); and that he definitely was not Management Material. They suggested that he take up whatever art was most attractive to him.

Clem, becoming less agitated, less elated, and more *conscious of detail* all the time, as the stuff in the tomato juice continued to mutate his nervous system, decided that he was one among possibly many thousands of subjects in a consciousness-expansion project being carried on by extraterrestrials.

Within a year he had written a symphony, which he decided was not very good, and had changed his religion ten times, without learning much in the process. He had also read his way through every volume of the *Encyclopaedia Britannica,* looking for clues as to what the hell was *really* going on.

Whoever was behind this experiment (and he was no longer quite sure they were necessarily extraterrestrials) seemed to have left a stream of grossly obvious Hints throughout every field of human knowledge. The stuff in the tomato juice was what theologians would call a gratuitous grace, but that was the only gratuitous part of it. You had to figure out, on your own, who They were, what They were up to, and what you should do about it.

The last thing you should do about it, Clem knew, was to *talk* about it, to the ordinary people who hadn't been given the stuff in the tomato juice. They would just think you were weird.

Clem had a list of people from history who (he figured) had probably been given the stuff in the tomato juice. The list started out with Jesus Christ, of course, and included a lot of the usual Suspects (Buddha, Michelangelo, Walt Whitman, Leonardo da Vinci), but it had quite a few that ordinary people would never have included, like Lewis Carroll and H. P. Lovecraft and General E. A. Crowley, the discoverer of the North Pole, and Joshua Abraham Norton, who in San Francisco in 1852 declared himself Emperor of the United States, Protector of Mexico, and King of the Jews.

For years Clem had tried to find others on the same neurological wavelength as himself. He had joined, and eventually been kicked out of, the Fortean Society, Mensa, the Rosicrucians, the Center for UFO Studies, and the ultra-secret SSFTASS (Secret Society for the Abolition of Secret Societies). He was too far-out for all of them.

A typical bit of Clem's musings from this period reads as follows:

Everything that exists has a cause. Since the universe exists, it must have a cause, and atheists are just being stubborn and pigheaded when they deny this. The cause of the universe is traditionally called God.

So far I sound as if I never left Little Rock.

But, it seems to me, the logic of the above is so sound, so clear, so indisputable (damn the atheists! it *is* indisputable) that it is only cowardice to drop it at this point, when it is beginning to prove illuminating.

Since God exists, God must have a cause. For clarity, let us call this cause God$_2$. [Why do the theologians always stick at this logical step? Cowardice and Fear of the Unknown, probably.]

Since God$_2$ exists, God$_2$ must have a cause.

At this point, everybody gives up and goes back to simple theism or simple atheism. Let us bravely push on:

Since God_n exists, God_n must have a cause, namely God_{n+1}.

Since $God_{infinity}$ exists, $God_{infinity}$ must have a cause, namely $God_{infinity+1}$.

What's wrong with this? It may look funny, but if it's logical it must be true.

I wonder what was in the tomato juice?

Some sort of molecules. Tomato juice is made up of molecules. And my brain is made up of molecules. So, then, the molecules of the stuff in the tomato juice got together with the molecules in my brain, and they've been having a ball ever since. And $God_{infinity+1}$ emerged.

But to carry on logically, following pure reason wherever it leads, $God_{infinity+1}$ must have a cause, namely $God_{infinity+2}$.

And so on, to $God_{infinity+infinity}$.

It has no end—not at infinity, not at double infinity, not at triple infinity, not at an infinity of infinities!!!

And, most beautiful of all, we have it on the authority of Jesus and all the other mystics that God is within. Therefore God_2 is within, and God_3, and so on to $God_{infinity+infinity+1}$, etc.

This is why you can think about yourself, and think about yourself thinking about yourself, and think about yourself thinking about yourself thinking about yourself, etc., to infinity and beyond.

Awareness is a trans-infinite regress, but I really ought to go lie down for a while before I get too excited. For a moment, there, I thought I knew what the hell was *really* going on.

Eventually, he organized his own society for the investigation and elucidation of "what the hell is *really* going on around here." He called it the Warren Belch Society, after the famous Old West lawman who won every gunfight because on each occasion when he confronted a shoot-out, his opponents' guns had mysteriously jammed.

The people Clem recruited were not the sort who would attribute Marshal Belch's phenomenal good luck to "coincidence"; nor would they be satisfied by metaphysical labels like "synchronicity" or "psychokinesis."

They assumed the extraterrestrials had some obscure cosmic reason for *protecting* Warren Belch.

On the day when Justin Case got tired wondering about Joe Malik's mysterious Last Communication and tried (unsuccessfully) to find out what it meant, Clem Cotex got tired wondering about the Invisible Hand Society. He marched down the hall, opened their door, and walked into a tiny but tastefully decorated reception room.

The wall to the right was adorned with a large gold dollar sign: **$**, emblazoned with the initials T.A.N.S.T.A.G.I. The wall to the left had a giant reproduction of the famous Steinberg cartoon of a little fish about to be eaten by a slightly bigger fish, which, in turn, was about to be eaten by a still bigger fish, which also was about to be eaten by an even bigger fish, and so on, to the border of the cartoon and evidently, beyond that, to infinity.

There was nobody in the room.

Clem looked around, a bit uncertainly.

SDATE YOUR BIZNIZ PLEEZ, said a computeroid voice, evidently out of the ceiling.

"Uh I'd like to see the head man or ah the head woman as the case may be," Clem stammered.

THAD WOULD BE DOKTOR RAUSS ELYSIUM, the computer said. HE IZ NOT IN THE OFFIZ TODAY.

"Oh ah tell him Clem Cotex called," Clem said, edging toward the door.

He suddenly didn't want to investigate the Invisible Hand any further, while he was alone. *Some other time,* he thought, *when I have some friends with me.*

YOUR MEZZAGE HAS BEEN RECORDED, the voice droned behind him as he fled the scene.

FALLING GIRDERS

The apprehension of the Real can only be compared
to a radiance or illumination because it is a revelation
of part of the coherence of the Divine Act of Creation.

—Pope Stephen, *Integritas,*
Consonantia, Claritas

Mary Margaret Wildeblood, Manhattan's bitchiest literary
critic, was getting just a tiny bit spiflicated. She was working
on her fifth martini, in fact.

"Mailer can't write," she said argumentatively. "None of
them can write. We haven't seen a real writer since Raymond Chandler."

"Um," said her companion noncommittally. He was Blake
Williams, tall, gray-bearded, eclectic: an alleged anthropologist (at least his degree was in anthropology) who
wrote and speculated wildly about dozens of sciences. Nobody knew whether he was a genius or just the most erudite
crank in the academic world.

"What do you mean, '*um*'?" Mary Margaret demanded
truculently. "I was talking nonsense just to see if you were
listening."

They were in the Three Lions bar on U.N. Plaza.

"Well, in fact, I was listening," Dr. Williams said urbanely. "You were comparing Mailer and Chandler, to the
disadvantage of Mailer. However, I admit my attention was
also wandering a bit. I was thinking about the Hollandaise
Sauce enigma." He was on his fifth martini, too.

"What's that?" Mary Margaret asked. Yet the martinis
must have been getting to her, because she did not wait for
his answer and announced, in the voice of Discovery, "The
best short story ever written is by John O'Hara."

70

"It was a case of food poisoning," Dr. Williams said. "A bunch of people got poisoned by some contaminated Hollandaise Sauce." Yet he looped back courteously and asked, "What short story?"

The robot who used the name "Frank Sullivan" came in and took a table near them. He was accompanied by Peter Jackson, the Black associate editor of *Confrontation* magazine.

"I forget the title," Mary Margaret said. "It was about a car salesman who has a very good day, makes some really topnotch sales, and stops at a bar to celebrate before going home. He has one drink after another and doesn't get home until after midnight, and *then* get this *and then* he goes and gets his rifle from the den and . . ."

"Oh I read that," Dr. Williams said. "It isn't a short story, it's a novel. Called um ah er *Appointment in Samara.* And he doesn't use a rifle. He gasses himself in his car."

"Damnedest case I ever heard of," pseudo-Sullivan said. "The Ambassador has been on *morphine* ever since."

"No," Mary Margaret said impatiently. "That was what the character in *Appointment in Samara* did, yes, everybody knows that one, but I'm talking about a *short story* O'Hara wrote much later, maybe thirty years later. In the short story, dammit what *is* the title, in the short story . . ."

"Wigged?" pseudo-Sullivan cried. "We thought we'd have to put him in a straitjacket."

"In the short story," Mary Margaret plowed on, noting that Williams was listening to the robot, "the salesman takes the rifle and goes to his bedroom and puts the rifle to his head . . ." She paused.

It worked. "And?" Williams asked, still wondering a bit about the Hollandaise Sauce mystery and why the Ambassador wigged.

"And his wife wakes up," Mary Margaret concluded, "and she says, 'Don't.' And he doesn't."

"He was hopping all around the room like a chicken on acid and making gargling and choking noises," the "man" called "Frank Sullivan" went on.

"He doesn't?" Williams cried.

"That's the point," Mary Margaret said. "You see, like the character in the *Samara* novel, this man goes right to the edge, he looks over the abyss, and then he pulls back at the last moment. Because his wife speaks to him."

"So it's a love story," Williams said. "Very sneaky and indirect, typical of O'Hara, but still a love story. He decides to continue carrying his burden, whatever it is, for the sake of the woman he loves."

"Well, how much will *Confrontation* pay for this?" pseudo-Sullivan demanded.

"No, it's more complicated than that," Mary Margaret argued. "The motive for the attempted suicide is never explained. Just like the motive for the real suicide in the *Samara* novel is never explained."

"Does it need to be explained?" Williams drawled, waving at the waiter for another martini. "If I were trapped into selling cars for a living, I'd think of blowing my head off occasionally."

"Yes but," Mary Margaret said. "Most people never see the emptiness of their lives the way these two characters of O'Hara's do. That's the Turn of the Screw. It's like the parable Sam Spade tells Brigid O'Shaughnessy in *The Maltese Falcon*. How he was hired to find a real estate salesman who'd disappeared . . ."

"A salesman again," Williams noted. "We are toying with synchronicity. When does Arthur Miller come on the scene?"

"Wait," Mary Margaret said. "It gets weirder. This salesman, in Spade's story, just went out to lunch one day and never returned. No evidence of foul play, no suicide note, *nada*. Years pass, and his wife wants to marry again, so she hires Spade to prove the salesman is really dead. Spade digs around and finds the salesman alive in another town, with a new name and a new family. He explains to Spade what happened when he went out to lunch that day and simply disappeared. A girder fell from a building under construction—you want to talk about synchronicity?—and almost killed him. It missed by only a few feet. It was like a Satori experience."

"A WHAT???" Peter Jackson, the Black editor, cried in astonishment at the next table.

Mary Margaret and Blake were both hooked; they looked deep, deep into their martini glasses as they strained not to miss pseudo-Sullivan's answer.

"A Rehnquist," the humanoid said.

"Jumpin' Jesus on a rubber crutch," Peter Jackson said.

"You're not putting me on? You mean right in the middle of the staircase . . ."

"Where the Ambassador had to see it when he came down to the reception," pseudo-Sullivan said. "A great big one, like Harry Reems' or what's-his-name's in the porn movies. With a pink ribbon around it. The *Company*," he stressed the word slightly, avoiding the initials, "thinks the K.G.B. did it. Believe me, the Ambassador hasn't been the same man since."

"Good Lord," Blake Williams said. "It's like your falling-girder story. Except in this case it's a falling Rehnquist . . . from the fourth Dimension, maybe." He was thinking that this was too wild to be a K.G.B. project and might involve the paranormal.

"Eva Gebloomenkraft was there," pseudo-Sullivan went on, "and kept trying to calm the Ambassador down, but he was just making those gargling noises and turning a funny kinda purple color. . . ."

"Eva Gebloomenkraft," Jackson said. "Isn't she that rich dame with the big Brownmillers who keeps getting eighty-sixed from nightclubs all over Europe?"

"Yeah," pseudo-Sullivan said. "A Jet Setter, you know? But she tried awfully hard to cheer up the Ambassador. Kept making little jokes about Freud's theories—Castration Anxiety and Rehnquist Envy and so on. . . . By then it had disappeared, by the way. But we know damned well the Ambassador didn't hallucinate it. Two of our men saw it, but they got distracted, trying to calm the Ambassador down when he first started jumping up and down and howling, 'In a pink ribbon, a pink ribbon!' and, 'What diseased mind could conceive it?' And stuff like that. . . ."

"It was as if this man's life was a watch," Mary Margaret said, picking up her own narrative. "And a jeweler had taken the back off and let him see how the gears worked. Nothing had meaning anymore in a universe where there's no good reason why a girder hits you or misses you."

"And Dashiell Hammett wrote this, you say?" Williams prompted. "It sounds very Existentialist."

Mary Margaret finished her sixth martini. "Hammett not only wrote it," she said, "he lived it. He spent ten years working for the Pinkertons when Class War was really War in this country. He knew that the girders fall on the just and the unjust."

"You mean he was a real detective who wrote about fictitious detectives?" Williams was off on his own tangent at once. "That's like Gödel's Proof. Or Escher painting himself painting himself . . ."

"Don't get too intellectual about it," Mary Margaret said. "You might miss the obvious."

RAINING CRABS AND PERIWINKLES

There is a heppy lend
Fur, fur away . . .

—George Herriman

One of the chief preoccupations of the Warren Belch Society was identifying the Mad Fishmonger.

This remarkable person had appeared, or had been alleged to have appeared, in Cromer Gardens, Worcester, England, on May 28, 1881. He, assisted by at least two dozen assistants, had scattered crabs and periwinkles all over the streets and in people's yards and even on the roofs of the houses.

The people of Cromer Gardens, obviously an unimaginative lot, could not imagine that a Mad Fishmonger had done this. They especially could not imagine how he (or maybe she?) had done it in broad daylight without being seen by anyone. They claimed the crabs and periwinkles had fallen out of the sky. Some even claimed, obviously under the mysterious influence of *"mob psychology,"* whatever that is, that they had seen the crabs and periwinkles falling.

They said it had been "raining crabs and periwinkles."

The scientists of the day, knowing full well that crabs and periwinkles do not fall out of the sky, claimed that the whole incident must have been an elaborate practical joke. One of them, writing in the prestigious *Nature* magazine, said that it must have been the work of "a Mad Fishmonger," although this writer neglected to explain how the Mad Fishmonger did it all without anybody seeing him.

This notion came under the scrutiny of a man named Charles Fort in the 1920s. Fort, who obviously had been given some of "the stuff in the tomato juice," although not as much of it as Clem Cotex got, refused to believe in the Mad Fishmonger. Fort, in fact, heaped all sorts of ridicule and derision upon the Mad Fishmonger. He said the Mad Fishmonger was the kind of strained hypothesis people invent when they don't want to acknowledge the obvious—the obvious being, to Fort, that on that day, in Cromer Gardens, crabs and periwinkles did fall out of the sky for some damned reason or other.

Clem Cotex had believed in Charles Fort for a long time—until he got kicked out of the Fortean Society for having weird ideas. Then he re-thought the whole Cromer Gardens Mystery, and since the "stuff" in the tomato juice was still working on his brain, he decided he did believe in the Mad Fishmonger, after all.

The Mad Fishmonger, he decided, was one of T.H.E.M. That was his name for the gang who handed out funny tomato juice and did other weird things like that. T.H.E.M. stood for They Have Everybody Mindwarped.

Clem was now an agnostic—and getting more agnostic all the time, as the funny tomato juice continued to mutate his neurons. He had no dogmas about T.H.E.M. They might be the Nine Unknown Men of Hindu Lore, or the Bavarian Illuminati, or the esoteric Network that computer programmers spoke of in hushed whispers, or they might even be the C.I.A.—without Tobias Knight's inside experience, Clem had deduced on his own that eveything published about the C.I.A. might be part of a *cover* or *screen* invented by themselves, and therefore he doubted that they were actually organized in 1948. They might have been around since Atlantis, and the story that they were part of the Unistat government, created during the Cold War, could be just another myth to hide their true purposes.

Clem even suspected that the Invisible Hand Society might be a front for T.H.E.M. That's why he couldn't bring himself to go back to their office alone, and kept procrastinating about getting a group together to go there with him.

He even thought, at times, that the Mad Fishmonger and

all the rest of T.H.E.M. might be agents of Silent Tristero's Empire.

This idea was plausible to him because he knew damned well he was living in a novel. That had been one of his first discoveries, in the first few hours after drinking the tomato juice.

SINCERITY IN SPELVINS

I'd rather have my mail delivered by Lockheed than ride in a plane built by the post office department.

—Bartholemew Gimble

Dr. Dashwood went out to dinner that night with Dr. Bertha Van Ation, the astronomer from Griffith Observatory who had discovered the two planets beyond Pluto.

They ate at Bernstein's Fish Grotto, the best seafood restaurant in San Francisco, which was becoming famous at that time for giving free meals to writers who plug it in their books, a tradition that had begun a few years earlier when they were prominently featured in the funniest science-fiction novel of 1981.

"Welcome to Bernstein's Fish Grotto," said the waiter. "I hope you enjoy the food."

"I always enjoy the food at BERNSTEIN'S FISH GROTTO!" Dashwood shouted.

"Why are you shouting?" Dr. Van Ation asked.

"I don't know," Dashwood said. "Something just sort of . . . came over me. . . ."

"Well, *Bernstein's Fish Grotto* is certainly worth shouting about," Dr. Van Ation said, in a low but intense voice.

Dashwood ordered a Manhattan with Southern Comfort—a combination that had never occurred to him before. He wondered how the idea got into his head—and Dr. Van Ation decided to try the same.

"Goethe said, *'Man muss entweder der Hammer oder der Amboss sein'*—you must be the hammer or the anvil," said a voice in the next booth.

"Mmm," Bertha Van Ation said. "This *is* good." She was sampling her Manhattan with Southern Comfort.

"Of course, he was just being melodramatic," the voice in the next booth said. "As an artist he must have known there are states in which you are *both* the hammer and the anvil—there's no either/or about it. That's the creative fire."

"So what's new in astronomy?" Dr. Dashwood asked.

"Uh?" Bertha said. "Oh, sorry, I was eavesdropping on the next booth."

"The hammer and the anvil," Dashwood said. "I heard him, too. Must be a poet. They tell me we have more poets 'of anthology rank,' whatever that is, than any other city in America."

"Like the *Hammersklavier* sonata," said a new voice, a feminine one, in the adjoining booth. "Beethoven was both the hammer and the anvil there. Maybe he even intended the pun. He read Goethe, didn't he?"

"Read him?" asked the first voice. "They knew each other. Would have been friends, if two egomaniacs could become friends."

"This is my favorite vice," Bertha whispered. "Listening in on the conversation at the next table."

"It sure sounds as if he had that idea in mind," the feminine voice said. "Is there any other piano piece where the pianist literally has to hammer away at the keys like that?"

"This is weird," Dashwood whispered. "I got a crank letter today—we get them by the ton at Orgasm Research, as you can imagine—and it was all about the *Hammersklavier*."

"My, what erudite cranks you attract," Bertha whispered. "The cranks who write to us, at Griffith, are mostly illiterate farmers who have seen UFO's."

"They went walking on the street once," the man in the next booth boomed. "And everybody kept bowing to them. Goethe finally said, 'I find all this ostentatious honor a bit embarrassing.' And you know what Ludwig said? He said, 'Don't let it bother you. It is *me* they are honoring.'"

The woman's silvery laugh had golden highlights of hashish in it. "That's Beethoven for you," she said.

Suddenly the two arose; they had evidently paid their check already and had been lingering over their coffee. Dr. Dashwood and Dr. Van Ation, without being conspicuous about it, looked them over as they left. They were both Chinese.

"That's San Francisco for you," Dashwood said.

"I bought a Vivaldi record the other day," Bertha said.

"It was made by a classical group in Japan, and they played his *Four Seasons* music on Japanese instruments. It sounded remarkably like the harpsichord he wrote it for."

"M," Dashwood nodded. "And we've got all these kids playing sitars and trying to sound like Ravi Shankar."

"The arts and sciences have always been international," Bertha said. "It's only our damned politics that remain nationalistic. To our sorrow."

"Mn." Dashwood nodded again. "But, as I was asking you a while ago, what's new in astronomy?"

"Well," Bertha said intensely, leaning forward, "the universe is turning out to be a hell of a lot bigger than we thought even three or four years ago. . . ."

At the other end of the room, seated at a table that gave a good view of Dashwood, the Continental Op was enjoying swordfish steak. He enjoyed it even more when he reminded himself that it could go on the expense account.

He owed this good fortune to the fact that Dashwood did not know his face yet.

Outside and across the street, Tobias Knight was dining on doughnuts and coffee from a deli, and bemoaning the fact that this typically warm San Francisco day had turned into a typically cold San Francisco night.

He owed this exile in the cold to the fact that Dashwood *did* know his face.

In Washington, Simon Moon had gone cruising at a bar called the Easter Basket. He had there picked up a young boy named Marlon Murphy, who had long blond hair and girlish mannerisms, both of which were qualities Simon appreciated.

They had gone back to Simon's pad and smoked some hash. Then they rapped for a while, and Simon learned that Marlon was working on a Master's in social psych, had a father who was a cop in San Francisco, and was a member of Purity Of Ecology.

Simon decided not to hold the last fact against the boy.

When they went to bed, Simon was the more aggressive at first, Briggsing young Marlon with slurping passion. But they soon turned it into a game, and each one would Briggs the other for a while, always stopping when it seemed one of them might reach Millett. After an hour of this, they were both on hair-trigger, and could restrain themselves no longer. Simon began to Bryant Marlon and they both started howling and panting and moaning until the bedroom began to sound like the Lion House at the zoo around mating time.

It was Simon Moon's idea of a great evening.

Dr. Dashwood was explaining the three dimensions of Briggsing to Dr. Van Ation, over coffee, at the other end of the continent.

"There just can't be any science without dimension," Dashwood said earnestly. "Pechner was the pioneer, psychometrics, what tastes sweeter than what and that sort of stuff. Primitive, of course, but it was the beginning of the quantification of the subjective, and my work could have followed immediately from his, except," he sighed, "you know how it is, fear and prejudice prevented the application of these methods to sex for a long time."

Dr. Van Ation nodded somberly.

"Sincerity we measure in Spelvins on a scale of 0 to 10," Dashwood went on, totally absorbed in his subject. "Hedonism in Lovelaces—we've been lucky there; subjects are able to distinguish 16 gradations. Finally, there's the dimension of Tenderness—we find 0 to 7 covers that, so that the perfect Steinem-Job, if I may use the vernacular, would consist of 10 Spelvins of Sincerity, 16 Lovelaces of Hedonism, and 7 Havens of Tenderness."

"It certainly makes our work seem easy by comparison," Dr. Van Ation said. "Everything is so concrete and objective in astronomy."

"What does that mean?" Marlon Murphy asked idly.

Simon, propping himself up on a pillow, looked where the boy was pointing. It was a sticker attached to the console of Simon's home computer, and it was in gold and black, with a dollar sign over which were imprinted the letters:

T.A.N.S.T.A.G.I.

"Oh, that," Simon said. "It's the insignia of the Invisible Hand Society."

"What's it mean—T.A.N.S.T.A.G.I.?"

"There Ain't No Such Thing as Government Interference," Simon translated.

Marlon rolled over and stared at him. "What is it, some kind of paradox?"

Simon smiled in that infuriatingly serene way that the enlightened always smile when dealing with the unenlightened. "It's no paradox," he said. "It's a simple statement of fact."

Marlon moved a few inches away. "You're some kind of mystic?" he asked nervously. The only mystics he had met were on the West Coast, and they were all, in his opinion, bonkers.

"Yes," Simon said easily. "We in the Invisible Hand are mystics; but we are also scientists. Every one of us has an advanced degree in math or quantum physics or computer science or some such field. Our founder, Dr. Rauss Elysium, was an expert in gravitational geometro-dynamics—four-dimensional topology, and so on—before he got into General Systems Theory."

"And you people, with all that math and so on, have convinced yourselves that *the government doesn't really exist?*" Marlon was beginning to get an exciting idea: he would do his Master's on this Invisible Hand Society, as an illustration of the psychological law that the more brilliant a mind is, the more elaborate will be its delusory system if it snaps.

"That's it," Simon said calmly. "A chicken is the egg's way of making more eggs. Government is anarchy's way of making more anarchy. Let me explain. . . ."

"So they were all poisoned by Hollandaise Sauce," Mary Margaret prompted, finishing her seventh martini delicately.

Blake Williams was deciding that Mary Margaret was a damned good-looking woman, considering that she had been a man until six months ago. He was on his seventh martini, too, and Marjorie Main would have looked like a damned attractive woman to him by then, even made up to look like Humphrey Bogart's mother in *Dead End*.

"Yes," he said, "well, that's not the mystery. They were all rushed to a hospital, and had their stomachs pumped, and they survived. I don't remember what had contaminated the Hollandaise Sauce, but it doesn't really matter. That's not the mystery."

"Well, what is the mystery?" Mary Margaret prompted. She was Encouraging him to Talk, and that suddenly alarmed him. It meant only one thing: she was thinking of going to bed with him.

"Uh," he said, "the mystery was what happened later." He had been thinking she was attractive, yes, but that was fairly abstract; he hadn't *really* decided, and when you faced up to it, she was still partly male in his mind.

"What happened later?" she prompted.

Damn it! he thought. *I must have had one martini too many*. She was a woman now; no doubt about it. So what was the problem?

"They all came down with the same symptoms again," he said. "The next time they had food with Hollandaise Sauce." The problem was that they would not merely Potter Stewart; there would be a certain amount of foreplay naturally, and they would be Briggsing each other.

"Oh? It was a synchronicity—two cases of contaminated Hollandaise Sauce hitting the same people?" Mary Margaret prompted him again.

"Ah no, it was far weirder than that." What *was* the matter? He had Briggsed a lot of women in his time, and had been Briggsed by a lot of them—he always enjoyed a good Steinem-Job, God knows—but still . . . there was something a bit faggoty about it when the woman was an ex-man and still *partly* a man in your memory. "Ah," he repeated, damning those martinis, "you see, there was nothing wrong with the Hollandaise Sauce the second time. No contaminant at all. They weren't poisoned. They ah just had the *symptoms* of poisoning."

"That is weird," Mary Margaret said, wondering if he was getting so flustered because he had never been to bed with a transsexual before. Well, he was an anthropologist, wasn't he? He should regard it as an educational experience.

"Very weird," Blake Williams said, "because you can't explain it by conditioning theory. Conditioning is a slow process, remember, requiring many repetitions or ah reinforcements. That's how Pavlov's dog learned that *bell* means *food*—repetition after repetition after repetition. But the dog-level or reflex-level of these people had learned that *Hollandaise Sauce* means *poison* in only one exposure." He should regard it as an educational experience, he decided; after all, he was an anthropologist.

"Well, I never believed you could explain everything by conditioning theory," Mary Margaret said. "I'm a Humanist."

"That's all very well and good, I'm sure," Blake Williams said, "but ah scientifically the behavior in question was certainly not mediated through the rational circuits of the cortex and does require ah some sort of explanation. I mean, if it wasn't conditioning, what the Potter Stewart was it?"

"Mmm," said Mary Margaret. "Mmm? How about imprinting?"

"What?" Dr. Williams looked, for a moment, like the Ambassador finding the Rehnquist on the stairs.

"Imprinting," Mary Margaret said. "When an animal learns something all-at-once-in-a-flash. Isn't that called imprinting?"

Williams stared.

"I think you've got it," he said finally. "How would you ah like to go up to my apartment and discuss this further?"

He was suddenly madly in love with her. She had given him a New Idea.

ATTIS

TERRAN ARCHIVES 2803:

The Syrian vegetation-god Attis castrated himself as a sacrifice to the great Mother Goddess, Kybele. His followers, in imitation of Attis, also castrated themselves. The cult eventually infiltrated Rome and had a strong influence on the early Christian Church, where Origen, a very influential theologian, castrated himself in the manner of the Attis sect. Later, Christian priests took vows of celibacy, transferring the castration to a psychological realm. As late as the nineteenth century (some say on into the twentieth), a Gnostic Christian sect in Russia, the *skopsi,* continued to castrate themselves.

We have found similar beliefs and practices on over 23,000,000 planets where the idea had been nurtured that *copulation is bad for the crops.* Contrariwise, we have found sex worship and phallic divinities on over 17,000 planets where shamans had believed that *copulation is good for the crops.* Earth was unique in having both these ideas inculcated by competing schools of primitive magicians and theologians. In fact, almost a century before the Wilson Era, an English anthropologist, Sir James George Frazer, demonstrated, in an epochal twelve-volume work, *The Golden Bough,* that all conflicting systems of Terran religion were derived from one or the other of these two primitive shamanic ideas. The puritans were Attisian, following the cluster of ideas and associations that sprang from the belief that copulation was harmful to the crops. The Tantrists, witches, and other underground cults with which our sublime Bard was evidently associated, if our surmise is correct, believed on the contrary that copulation was beneficial to the crops. It was due to the political power of the puritans that so much of *The Homing Pigeons* is written in code.

I'M STILL HERE

It is, then, only when the mind confronts the Real
without prejudgment that we can be liberated from
sin and error.

—Pope Stephen, *Integritas,*
Consonantia, Claritas

In San Francisco, Dr. Van Ation had been Briggsing Dr.
Dashwood for twenty minutes.

He sounded like a man at prayer. "Oh, God," he kept
repeating. "Oh, God, God, God . . ."

Dr. Van Ation was thoroughly enjoying herself. Dashwood had Briggsed her for forty minutes, during which she
reached Millett six times, and she was still purring with
gratitude.

"Oh, God, God, *God*," Dashwood croaked. as her
tongue continued to excite his Rehnquist.

In Washington, Old Iron Balls Babbitt was Potter Stewarting a young lady from the State Department's translation department.

She also sounded like a person in religious ecstasy. *"Mon
Dieu!"* she panted, *"Mon Dieu!* Oh oh oh ah! *Mon Dieu!"*

Old Iron Balls had a different imprint. "Potter Stewart,"
he kept growling, "Potter Stewart. Potter Stewart. Take it
in your Falwell, your Falwell, your Falwell . . ."

"And so," Simon Moon concluded, "government is just a glitch. A semantic hallucination."

"Mrn-mn," said Marlon Murphy.

Simon turned around and looked at the boy; and it was as he feared: Marlon was about eighty percent asleep. Simon had been lecturing virtually to himself for several minutes.

"Non Illegitimati carborundum," he muttered. It was his *mantra* against resentment, wrath, and other diseases of the ego.

He leaned over and kissed Marlon lightly on the ear.

"Mrn," Marlon mumbled.

Simon got up from the bed and padded into the living room, where he smoked a little more hash and remembered classrooms back in Chicago, beatings he had received for being intellectual and queer, the first boy he had ever Briggsed (wasn't his name Donald something?), the beauty of Russell's definition of number when he finally grasped it (the class of all classes that are similar), the first time he was Bryanted (he was afraid it would hurt), the strange out-of-book experience in New York on hash when he saw that the laws that govern us are partly grammatical and partly pure whimsy, and this was very good hash, indeed, because he could almost remember that experience: there was a universe where he was hetero and Furbish Lousewart was President; yes, this was very high-grade hash, indeed, and he almost believed it, and why not? The math certainly did imply such universes, and each universe could be like a book, each book a variation on the same theme, and the Author (if one dared to try to imagine such a Being) might even be in a meta-universe which had its own Author, and so on, to infinity. . . .

But then suddenly (hashish is full of surprises) Simon was weeping, remembering his father, old Tim Moon, who had been a Wobbly organizer all his life, and Tim was singing "Joe Hill" again:

> The copper bosses killed you, Joe
> I never died, said he

"Oh, Dad," Simon said aloud. "Why did you have to die, before I ever knew how much I loved you?" And suddenly he was all alone in an empty living room, weeping like an old man whose family and friends were all dead, holding his Social Security check and wondering: Where is the Federal bureau in charge of distributing love?

Which was absurd: Simon had lots of friends, and he was just being morbid.

"Oh, Dad"—he sniffled one more time—"I *miss* you."

And then he stopped crying and went and put the Fugs' record of "Rameses the Second Is Dead, My Love" on the stereo. And floated with the music and the hash into a Country-and-Western Egyptian paradise:

> He's walking the fields where the Blessed live
> He's gone from Memphis to Heeeeaav-en!

"Well?" Mary Margaret Wildeblood prompted, a bit impatiently. She was naked on Williams' bed and had been Lourding herself, not vigorously, just gently, very gently, not getting too excited yet, merely trying to get him excited.

"Just a minute just a minute," Williams said, sitting in his drawers on the side of the bed, one sock in his hand. It wasn't the transsex thing that was delaying him; he was still struggling with the New Idea she had given him back at the Three Lions. "It isn't just poisoning," he said absently. "*Anything* that shocks the whole neuro-endocrine system might do it. Yes, of course. Artificially induced imprint vulnerability."

Mary Margaret seized his hand and placed it firmly between her thighs. "Imprint that," she said coyly.

"Yes yes," he said, caressing her absently. "But just listen a minute. Orgasm does it um I think. No, just the first orgasm. Right? You keep repeating the pattern of the first orgasm. . . ."

"*I* don't," Mary Margaret said. "Just up there a bit, on my Atkinson there, *there*, ah Christ."

"Yes yes you don't and a lot of people I know don't," he said. "Yes. Um? But the people whose sexual patterns keep changing are a minority, certainly. They've changed their imprints somehow. Um. Yes, yes. Oh, my God!"

"What *is* it?" Mary Margaret was becoming cross; his hand had stopped moving entirely.

"Sorry," he said, resuming the gentle stimulation on her Atkinson and the outer lips of her Feinstein. "I just realized, some people keep changing their ideas, too. They've loosened the semantic imprints. My God, that's why conditioning theory is inadequate. Don't you see the conditioned reflexes are built onto the imprints . . ."

"God God God oh sweet Jesus God"

"It's a shock to the whole system. People who've had near-death or clinical death experiences. Shipwrecked sailors. And oh Jesus I call myself an anthropologist and I never got it before, rites of initiation of course that's what they're all about of course making new imprints. . . ."

"Oh God oh God darling darling"

"Yes yes, I love you, new imprints of course, yes yes are you coming oh my little darling"

"God God GOD!!!"

"Ah sweet little darling was it good? Ah yes you look so sweet now there's nothing as lovely as that post-Millett expression but about those imprint circuits—"

"Shut up and Briggs me *please* darling"

And so, still reflecting on shock and imprint vulnerability and the changing of sexual-semantic imprints, Blake Williams began Briggsing a person who had been masculine for almost all the years they had known each other, wondering just how queer this was, really.

"*Mon Dieu* oh oh oh ah," the lady from State was still moaning.

"Potterstewartpotterstewartpotterstewart," Old Iron Balls growled. "You love it don't you you love it you love it . . ."

"Incidentally," Dr. Dashwood asked, "what do *you* think the *Hammersklavier* is all about?"

Bertha Van Ation and he were sitting at the kitchen table now, sipping a little peach brandy he had found still remaining in the cabinet, and munching Ritz crackers.

Dr. Van Ation brushed some auburn hairs back from her forehead. "The Black Hole," she said promptly.

"Ah you mean he was feeling dragged down into something he couldn't escape?" Dr. Dashwood suddenly remembered he wanted to look up Jan (or was it Hans?) Zelenka.

"No, not that aspect of it." Bertha munched and frowned thoughtfully. "The suspension of all the cosmological laws. The end of space. The end of time. The end of causality."

Dashwood smiled. "Some people thought it was the end of music when it was first performed," he said. "You might be on the right track."

"Why thank you sir said she." Bertha grinned. "You really think I'm dragging my own astronomy into the music department."

"You have every right to," he said. "We all see and hear through our own filters. To me, the *Hammersklavier* sounds like an unsuccessful attempt at Tantric sex. And the *Seventh* and *Eighth Symphonies* sound like monumentally successful attempts. That's me dragging my own speciality into the music department."

"You are a doll."

"And you're a *living* doll."

"Isn't sex great?"

"If God invented anything better," Dashwood said, quoting an old proverb and adapting it to the Feminist age, "She kept it to Herself."

"And how did I score on your scale?"

"Ten Splevins of Sincerity, 16 Lovelaces of Hedonism, and 7 Havens of Tenderness. No, make that 8 Havens. You went off the scale."

In Hollywood, Carol Christmas, the Blonde Goddess of everybody's fantasies, was sleeping alone for once.

She was still involved in 250,000,000 sex acts every hour.

The quantum perturbations pulsed gently through her atoms, stimulating her molecules, rejuvenating her cells, providing a very satisfactory Trip for her whole neuro-endocrine system, and enriching her dreams vastly.

It was perfect Tantric sex, and she wasn't even consciously aware of it.

This was happening to her, and had been happening to her since the release of *Deep Mongolian Steinem-Job*, because she *was* the Blonde Goddess in so many fantasies.

All over the world, as she slept and even while she was awake in the daytime, the quantum inseparability principle (QUIP) stimulated her gently, because all over the world, every hour, 250,000,000 lonely men were Lourding themselves while looking at photographs of her.

Back in New York, Polly Esther Doubleknit was wandering around her apartment stark-naked.

Her lover of the evening was sound asleep in the bedroom, but Polly Esther was wakeful and thinking of twenty dozen things at once, like the Second Oswald in Hong Kong and whether fish ever get seasick and how splendidly heavenly it had felt when her lover's tongue was up inside her Feinstein and what was the name of the third Andrews Sister—Maxine and Laverene and *who?*—and Silent Tristero's Empire and why so many things come in threes, not just Maxine and Laverne and what's-her-name but Curly and Larry and Moe; and Tom, Dick, and Harry; and Noah's three sons, Ham, Shem, and Japhet; and Groucho, Chico, and Harpo; and Brahma, Vishnu, and Shiva; and Past, Present, and Future; and Breakfast, Lunch, and Dinner; and the three witches in *Macbeth;* and the three brothers who start on the same quest in all the old fairy tales; and the Executive, the Legislative, and the Judiciary; and of course the Big Three, Pops, J.C., and Smokey; and maybe she should cut down on those diet pills; it was absurd to be wandering around at three in the morning thinking in threes.

And then there was up-down, back-forward, and right-left, the three dimensions in space; and Wynken, Blynken, and Nod; and the Three Wise Men, Whozit and Whatzisname and Melchior; and Peter, Jack, and Martin, the three brothers in Swift's *Tale of a Tub;* and Peter, Paul, and Mary; and the Kingston Trio; and Friends, Romans, Countrymen, which was not only a triad, but a progressive triad, one beat, two beats, three beats, one, two, three, just like that, and she would definitely cut down on the diet pills.

Polly Esther finally put a record on the stereo, turning the volume down to low so as not to waken her lover in the bedroom.

She picked the *Hammersklavier* sonata, not out of coincidence or propinquity or even synchronicity, but just because it was her favorite of Beethoven's piano pieces. It was her favorite because she couldn't understand it, no matter how often she played it. It was the musical equivalent of a Zen koan to her, endlessly fascinating because endlessly enigmatic.

The stark, discordant opening bars drove all wandering threesomes out of her mind, narrowing her attention to Ludwig's urgent if incomprehensible universe of structured sound. She was swept into it again, as always, swept along by emotions so deep and yet so austere that nobody has ever been able to name them. Once she had invited the world's three most admired concert pianists to a party, just so she could ask each of them, privately, what they thought the *Hammersklavier* meant. As she expected, she had gotten three wildly conflicting answers. Another time, she had ordered every book in print about Beethoven from Doubleday's on Fifty-third Street at Fifth Avenue and looked up *Hammersklavier* in the index of each. She got forty-four different opinions that way.

The music hammered and surged along, carrying her through pain and frustration and loneliness to land, again and again, at things beyond such simple feelings, things that she sometimes felt were extraterrestrial or non-Euclidean or somehow beyond normal human perception. There are some kinds of knowledge, Ludwig had once claimed, that can only be expressed in music, not in any other art, not in science or philosophy. This was the most arcane of such knowledge, Ludwig's most intimate secret, and maybe you weren't entitled to understand it until you had been to the strange dark places of the psyche out of which he had created it.

It was the childbirth process, of course—and Polly Esther did not consider it a miracle that Ludwig could understand that, he was so obviously bi, at least empathetically—the labor pains going on and on until the act of creation seemed impossible, you would never get there, and yet somehow even in the blocked hopeless feeling you *were* getting there; and it was all the terrors of his childhood, all those cruel beatings by his alcoholic father, remembered and not forgiven, never forgiven; but it was also that cold, analytical, almost scientific side of Ludwig, remorselessly following his experiment to its inexorable conclusion: he had discovered or rediscovered that the piano is, among other things, a percussion instrument and he was following the logic of that insight, as he followed every musical idea, to wherever it led him, to whatever abyss.

And, after thinking all that, Polly Esther knew she still didn't understand the *Hammersklavier;* but as it banged and howled to its defiant conclusion, she got a flash of one aspect she had never registered before. It was the last scene of *Papillon,* when after twelve years of horror, Steve McQueen finally escapes from Devil's Island on his homemade raft of coconut shells and floats off into the Atlantic, as Ludwig floats off at the end of the *Hammersklavier,* shouting to the hostile sea and the indifferent sky:

"I'M STILL HERE, you sons-of-bitches!"

And, after that, Polly Esther was cleaned out, drained, purified; no more triangles haunted her. She turned off the stereo, yawned contentedly, and padded back to her bed.

Her lover was still sleeping, twisted around in the covers so that her right leg stuck out, decorated with goose pimples from the cold air. Polly Esther re-arranged the bedding to cover the girl, and climbed in beside her, hugging her tenderly once, but not enough to waken her.

Then there were only a few remembered bars of the *Hammersklavier* and one more trio drifted up (Wyatt, Morgan, and Vergil, the Earp brothers), and then Polly Esther slept.

But Mary Margaret Wildeblood woke up suddenly, hardly noticing Williams snoring beside her.

"My God," she said. "I wonder if it was Ulysses. . . ."

The
Second
Loop

Art imitates nature.
    —Aristotle

Nature imitates art.
    —Oscar Wilde

WHAT—ME INFALLIBLE?

The first entry of Sin into the mind occurs when, out of cowardice or conformity or vanity, the Real is replaced by a comforting lie.

—Pope Stephen, *Integritas, Consonantia, Claritas*

Dr. Dashwood, as usual, began Friday by scanning the mail.

The first letter said:

THIS IS AN ENTIRELY NEW KIND OF CHAIN LETTER! ! !

We represent the Fertilizer Society of Unistat. It will not cost you a cent to join. Upon receipt of this letter, go to the address at the top of the list and Burger on their front lawn. You won't be the only one there, so don't be embarrassed.

Then make five copies of this letter, leaving the top name off and adding your name and address at the bottom. Send them to five of your best friends and urge them to do the same. You won't get any money, but within five weeks, if this chain is not broken, you will have 3,215 strangers Burgering on your lawn. [Here Comes Everybody!]

Your reward next summer will be the greenest lawn on the block.

DO NOT BREAK THIS CHAIN! Everybody who has broken it has within five days suffered acute, prolonged, and inexplicable constipation which responds to no known laxative and requires, in each case, intervention of the apple-corer or its surgical equivalent.

Budweiser N. Kief
2323 N. Clark
Chicago, Illinois 60611

Occupant
P. O. Box 666
Bad Ass, Texas 23023

G. Neil's Artificial Life & Pipe Storage Co.
401 N. 27th
Billings, Montana 59101

Mystery Whizz and Whats-It Works
210 E. Olive
Bozeman, Montana 59715

Dynamite Dave's Phosphate Soda and Kangaroo Stand
Kibbutz Palmahim
Doar Rishon, Israel

Ethyl's Chocolate Shoppe & Nonphenomena
    Foundation
242 West Lincoln,
Anaheim, California 92805

Dr. Dashwood made a mistake. He assumed this was another hoax by the enigmatic Ezra Pound.

Polly Esther Doubleknit was a devout Roman Catholic and went to Confession that Saturday.

"I did a naughty-naughty with a Secretary again," she said.

"How shocking," said her Confessor in a profoundly bored tone. "Was she cute?"

"She was an absolutely adorable little blonde creature."

"I hope you both enjoyed yourselves," said the priest. "But why are you telling me about this hedonic little escapade?"

Polly Esther whispered, "I guess I feel guilty. I was raised Baptist, you know."

"But you're a Catholic now," the priest, Father Starhawk, said. "And as a convert, you probably know the theology better than people who were born into it. Now, tell me: What is a sin?"

"A sin," Polly Esther recited promptly, "is to knowingly hurt a sentient being."

"Except where it would be a greater sin, a greater hurt, to refrain," Father Starhawk went on. "That's why it's no sin to kill a virus, remember. Now, did you hurt your cute little blonde playmate?"

"No, of course not."

"Did you make her happy?"

"I think so," Polly Esther said wistfully. "She wants to see me again Monday night."

"Then I think you made her happy," Father Starhawk said. "How many times did she reach Millett?"

"Six or seven, I think."

"Then I'm *sure* you made her happy," the priest said kindly. "As a mere male, I must say I envy the female capacity for multiple Millett. Now, obviously, your little party with this Secretary was not harmful, but joyful. So it was not a sin, but the opposite of a sin, a work of virtue. And you know the teachings of Moral Theology well enough to understand that, so why are you wasting my time?"

"I guess it's just my Baptist upbringing," Polly Esther murmured.

"You must clear your mind of all superstition," the priest said, "because such nonsense muddies the intellect and keeps you from thinking clearly about Real moral issues. Now, do you have something Real to confess?"

"Yes," Polly Esther said nervously.

"Well?" Father Starhawk's jovial tone suddenly turned stern.

"I think some of my money comes from slum properties." Polly choked, then sighed deeply. It was a relief to say it, to have it out in the open.

"You *think?*" the priest cried angrily. "You haven't found out for sure? How long have you had this suspicion?"

"Since about a week ago last Thursday."

"And what efforts have you made to find the facts about this grave matter, which may be, I remind you, a mortal sin?"

Polly Esther trembled. "I tried," she said, "but the way corporations are these days . . . I get twelve different stories every time I ask the lawyers . . . but I really think we own some of the worst parts of Newark."

The priest was silent a long time. "It's my fault," he said finally. "I was never strict enough with you. What is the first moral law about money?"

"To ensure that no human being was hurt in acquiring it, and if anyone was hurt, to return the money to them and make whatever other restitution is morally necessary."

"To ensure," Father Starhawk repeated solemnly. "Saint Francis Xavier said that many centuries ago, a great and holy saint, and he specifically instructed priests to be certain that nobody received Absolution until they had given up all monies acquired from usury or other social injustices. That was long before Pope Stephen, my child, and it is the moral backbone of the Church. I cannot give you Absolution until you have examined your conscience on this matter and made whatever change is morally necessary."

"I'll have a special Board meeting and get to the bottom of it," Polly Esther said. "Thank you, Father, for restoring my vision of Reality."

"That is the function of the Church," Father Starhawk said.

And then he added, softly:

"Pray for me, please. I am a sinner, also."

Father Starhawk was a Cherokee Indian and a Stephenite.

The Stephenites were the most radical of all the Catholic clergy and made even the Neo-Jesuits, under General Berrigan, seem like milkwater liberals by comparison. There was virtually no nation on Earth which didn't have several Stephenites in prison for what the Stephenites called "following the laws of God rather than the laws of Man."

Members of the Stephenite order absolutely refused to countenance any behavior that fell short of the ideals in the late Pope Stephen's encyclicals on Social Justice; and what the Stephenites would not countenance, they would resist. It was the passive, nonviolent nature of their resistance that made the Stephenites so troublesome to persons in authority; it is impossible to jail nonviolent idealists without a large part of the world sympathizing with them.

Father Starhawk had served three terms himself, for passively resisting Unistat's wars against Cuba, Puerto Rico, and the People's Republic of Hawaii.

Like all Stephenites, he wore the familiar lapel button with a photo of Pope Stephen, the famous black patch over his blind eye, and the sainted Pope's famous remark, "What—*me* infallible?"

Pope Stephen had totally revolutionized the Catholic Church during his brief five-year reign. Indeed, as the French feminist Jeanne Paulette Sartre said, "This one man has singlehandedly turned the most reactionary church on this planet into the most progressive."

It was due to Pope Stephen that the "social gospel," previously preached only by a minority of far-out Jesuits and worker-priests, became the official Vatican policy. By being the first to denounce Hitler and Mussolini, and excommunicating their supporters, Pope Stephen had knowingly risked the biggest rupture within the Church since the time of Luther; but, while nearly thirty percent of the Catholics in Germany and Italy continued to follow their national leaders, over seventy percent obeyed the Pope, and both dictators fell from power.

Adolf Hitler became a portrait painter again; and Benito Mussolini, deprived of power, returned to his early belief in anarchism and spent his declining years writing fiery journalism against all those who did manage to achieve and hold on to political power.

At the time of Pope Stephen's death in 1940, it was estimated that the wealth of the Vatican was less than ten percent of what it had been when he took the Chair of Peter, but its prestige about one thousand percent higher.

The Pope had spent ninety percent of the Vatican's wealth in projects for the abolition of poverty, disease, and ignorance.

Many regarded him as a saint, but Pope Stephen always tried to discourage that view. He ended every conversation with "I am a sinner, also," which became a habit with Stephenites; Father Starhawk, for instance, ended *all* his conversations that way, and also used it for the tagline of all his theological articles and his private correspondence.

It must be admitted, however, that the first Irish Pope did have his own brand of arrogance: he believed he was the best Latin stylist since Cicero, and was rather vain about his command of English, Italian, French, German, Spanish, Danish, and Hebrew, also. He was also convinced that he was a greater psychologist than James or Jung, and it was only when their names were mentioned that a tinge of uncharitable sarcasm would enter his speech.

Pope Stephen, in fact, had a habit of listening far more than he spoke, which led many to regard him as a bit aloof. Actually, he spoke little because he was so busy *observing*. This passion for studying other human beings had gradually turned him from a disputatious young intellectual into an almost pathologically sensitive middle-aged man, because the more he observed people, the more he liked them, and the more he liked them, the less able he was to bear seeing or hearing of injustice to anyone anywhere.

On one occasion, a learned and erudite French Cardinal said to the Pope, referring to the steady parade of visitors to the Vatican, "You must find most of these nonentities profoundly boring." He was making the usual mistake of interpreting the Pope's long silences as a sign of ennui.

"But—there are no bores," Stephen said, shocked.

"You are being paradoxical," the Cardinal chided.

"Not at all," the Pope said dogmatically. "I have never met a boring human being."

It was the only time anybody ever heard him pontificate.

It was due to Pope Stephen that every Catholic priest was not only allowed, but encouraged, to get married. "Living with the mystery of the feminine mind," he said, "is the best training for trying to cope with the greater mysteries of the Divine mind."

He himself had married a peasant girl from Galway, who was said to be barely literate, and his love for her was legendary.

Nobody knew what the Pope and his wife ever found to talk about, since she obviously did not share any of his intellectual interests.

Actually, with his wife, as with most of humanity, the Irish Pope spent most of his time listening, not talking.

Because of the liberality of his sexual views, the Irish Pope was still controversial among conservative Catholics, who claimed he was a pervert and were forever trying to have him posthumously excommunicated.

They also spread rumors about his private life, which had gained so much currency that whenever his name was mentioned somebody would mutter "garters, garters, garters."

Pope Stephen's whole philosophy was derived from a single sentence in Aquinas:

> *Ad pulchritudinem tria requiruntur:*
> *integritas, consonantia, claritas.*

Which may be rendered:

> Three things are required for beauty:
> wholeness, harmony, radiance.

It was Stephen's thought that the universe, as the product of a Great Artist, must be comprehensible in terms of *integritas, consonantia, claritas*—wholeness, harmony, radiance. Why, then, he asked himself, does it not appear so to the ordinary human mind? The only answer he could find was that *we are not paying attention*. We have not learned to observe closely enough. We do not have the Artist's eye for detail.

And so Pope Stephen paid very close attention to everything that entered his field of perception.

At the time of the Irish Pope's death in 1940, obituary writers all over the world compared him to every saint and sage in history: Buddha, Whitman, Plotinus, Rumi, Dante, Eckhart, John of Arc, St. Terrence of Avilla, and so on, and on; but the one who came closest to categorizing how Stephen's mind worked was an obscure Canadian professor of literature who wrote: "The only mind in history comparable to Stephen's was that of a fictitious character—Mr. Sherlock Holmes of Baker Street."

Like Tobias Knight, Pope Stephen had spent all his life "trying to find out what the hell was really going on," although he never expressed it that way.

He had decided that what was going on was that everybody was very carefully avoiding paying attention to what was going on.

The Stephenites called themselves "Seekers of the Real" and were always watching very closely to see what was going on. They all had posters in their rooms with the sainted Pope's famous remark: "If you don't pay attention to *every little detail,* you miss most of the jokes."

When Dr. Dashwood went out to lunch that day, he was stopped on the street by a haggard and wild-eyed minor bureaucrat who said his name was Joseph K.

"They have everybody mindwarped." Joseph K. said, clutching Dashwood's sleeve desperately.

"Yes, yes," Dashwood said, trying to disentagle himself. "But I really must hurry—"

"What are the charges against me?" Joseph K. demanded. "What are the charges against any of us? We all try to obey their rules, don't we? Of course we do; we know what will happen at the slightest, the most minute, the most *microscopic* infraction, do we not? Not that I mean to imply that they are wrong, necessarily, or unjust—you won't find any subversive literature or pornography in my room, I can assure you absolutely—no, certainly not *unjust* or in any way *unfair,* but it must be admitted that in the application of the rules, in the *application,* I say, they are sometimes over-finicky, a bit *strained* and literal, if you take my meaning."

"Certainly, certainly," Dashwood said, struggling to remove Joseph K.'s fingers from his sleeve. "But if you were to see a good counselor—not a psychiatrist, necessarily . . . I don't mean to imply—"

"We are all guilty," Joseph K. said flatly. "They have established so many rules, and recorded them in archives that the ordinary citizen cannot consult, that we must all, the most loyal and decent of us, stumble on a mere technicality occasionally. Not that I mean to assert that technicalities are not necessary, you understand, since it is important to spell out in detail the *exact* meaning intended in a statute, don't you agree, George?"

"Frank," Dashwood said automatically.

Joseph K. suddenly looked sly. "Oh," he said slowly. "You claim that you are not George Dorn? How clever of them, although I can't imagine how they persuaded you, but of course a man of your moral principles would not be *bribed,* certainly. They must have convinced you it was for my own good in some absolute metaphysical sense, right? Certainly. You would not work for them out of *malice,* would you?" He released Dashwood with a poignant, despairing gesture. "You mean well," he said. "They all mean well, I know. *But I am innocent,* I tell you!"

He backed away. "And you *are* George Dorn, and I am not deceived," he added bitterly.

Then he turned and ran.

PARAREALISME

Those who can only follow the old procreative routine in a nonprocreative revolutionary period are like foolish old men going out in the rain to a wooden privy when the cooperative has already established a progressive communal indoors bathroom.

—Mao Tse-tung, Interview with the
American Journalist Michael O'Donoghue,
April 14, 1972

The big news of the 1985 season in the art world was that François Loup-Garou had abandoned Neo-Surrealism and founded a new school of art called *Pararealisme*.

This was only partly the result of the Rehnquist in the Lobster Newburg; it was also a matter of economics.

For nearly a century it had been very important for an artist to belong to a "school," and it was even better to be the founder of a "school." This was not just a case of "In Union There Is Strength"; it was also a shrewd marketing strategy. It might take an individual painter ten or twenty years to be "discovered"—if he were original, it might take much longer, and he might not be alive to enjoy it—but when a School of Art was formed, that was News, and all members of the school were discovered simultaneously.

There had been an Impressionist school, a Post-Impressionist school, an Expressionist school, an Abstract Expressionist school, a Cubist school, a Futurist school, a Pop school and an Op school, and so on. François Loup-Garou had noticed that the commercial life of each school was getting shorter all the time, due to the accelerated intensity of competition: Neo-Surrealism was already being eclipsed, as an object of news and debate, by the Neo-Cubism of the American, Burroughs.

He decided it was time to launch a new school.

After the experience of the Rehnquist in the Lobster Newburg, *Pararealisme* seemed appropriate to him.

According to Standard Operating Procedure, he got a few friends together and they began issuing Proclamations denouncing all other schools (especially Neo-Cubism) as obsolete and reactionary. This got them into the Art Journals and into some newspapers.

Then they held their own first show, and that got them into the international news magazines.

They were news; it didn't really matter if their paintings were any good at all.

In fact, their paintings were rather good, in a fey sort of way.

They had revived traditional "representational" art (everything they did was as naturalistic as a news photograph), but with a difference that made a difference.

The largest canvas at the first Pararealiste show was Loup-Garou's own *What Do You Make of This, Professor?* An enormous work it was, covering two walls, bent in the middle on a special hinged frame. It showed a cerulean-blue sky, with hailstones: thousands and thousands of hailstones, six months' painstaking labor, and each hailstone had a tiny image of the Virgin Mary on it.

Puzzled viewers might have found some enlightenment in the First Pararealiste Manifesto:

> We of the Pararealiste movement, recognizing the meaninglessness of this chaos that fools call life, find the relevance of existence only in its monstrosities.
>
> But we are not Existentialists or anything of that sort, thank God; and besides, the perversities of humanity have grown boring. After the Fernando Poo Incident, what can a mere man do that will shock us? It is the *abnormalities of nature* that we find illuminating; that is what distinguishes us from sadists, New Leftists, and other intellectual hoodlums.

We are delighted that Pluto, Mickey, and Goofy are all at odd angles from the plane of the eight inner planets. We are thrilled with Bohr's great principle of Relativity, which shows that to look out into space is also to look backward in time. WE ARE THE DAY AFTER YESTERDAY!!!

Some said that the Pararealistes were even better at writing manifestos than at painting pictures; but they meant what they said. The hailstones in *What Do You Make of This, Professor?* were no image of dream or delirium— "We spit on surrealism! Fantasy is every bit as dreary as Logic! It is the REAL that we seek!" the First Manifesto had also declared. What Loup-Garou had so painstakingly depicted was an occurrence that actually happened at Lyons in 1920. Xeroxes of the old newspaper stories about the event ("PEASANTS SEE VIRGIN ON HAILSTONES") were distributed to the press, emphasizing again that Pararealistes only painted the real, or as they always wrote it, the REAL.

Little Pierre de la Nuit—Pierrot le Fou, he styled himself—was Loup-Garou's best friend and had contributed seventeen canvases to the first show. Magnificent, monstrous things they were, of course—flying saucers, all of them: blue and gold and silver and green and bright orange, shaped like doughnuts or boomerangs or ellipsoids or cones. Every one of them had been reported in the sky by somebody or other in the past forty years. Loup-Garou circulated news stories about each sighting, you can be sure, to demonstrate again Pararealisme's devotion to the REAL.

Then there was Jean Cul's *The Sheep-Cow;* some claimed it was the greatest of all Pararealiste paintings. It portrayed an animal half-sheep and half-cow, a veritable insult to the laws of genetics. Such an animal had been born in Simcoe, Ontario, in 1888. They circulated news stories about it.

All of this created so much international discussion that the Pararealistes immediately released a second Manifesto. (They had learned something about P.R. from the early surrealists.)

They denounced those who did not like their paintings as fools. They then denounced those who *did* like their paintings as damned fools, for liking them for the wrong reasons. They went on to fulminate against everybody in general:

> We renounce and hurl invective upon the rationalist conducting experiments in his laboratory. Every instrument he uses is a creation of human narcissism; it emerges from the human ego as Aphrodite from the head of Zeus. The rationalist imposes his own order on these instruments; they impose order on the data; and he then proclaims that the universe is as constipated and mechanistic as his own mind! What has this epistemological masturbation to do with the REAL?
>
> And we abominate and cast fulminations upon the irrationalist, also. Behold him in his drugged stupor, maddened by opium or hashish, gazing *inward* and depicting his childish dreams and nightmares on canvas. He is as limited by the human unconscious as the rationalist is by the human conscious. Neither of them can see the REAL!!!

It reads better in the original French. But it would have been a top news story if it hadn't been eclipsed by the singularly obscene "miracle" at Canterbury Cathedral that week.

The details of the alleged "miracle" had been censored and covered up by high Church officials from the very beginning. Newspapers, at first, printed only short items saying that something strange caused the Archbishop of Canterbury to turn a ghastly white during Mass and stumble so badly that he fell off the altar.

Of course, some cynics immediately assumed that His Eminence was as drunk as a skunk. There are always types like that, believing the worst of everybody.

Then the rumors started to circulate. Those who had been in the Cathedral said that the Most Reverend Archbishop had not so much stumbled as *jumped,* and that his expression was one of such fear and loathing that all present felt at once that something distinctly *eldritch* and *unholy* had invaded the church. Others, imaginative types and religious hysterics, claimed to have felt something cold and *clammy* moving in the air, or to have seen "auras."

By the time the rumors had gone three times around the United Kingdom and twice around Europe, there were details that came right out of the *Necronomicon* or the grim fictions of Stoker, Machen, Walpole. Horned men, Things with tentacles, and Linda Lovelace were prominently featured in these embroidered versions of the Canterbury Horror, as it was beginning to be called.

The press, of course, got more interested at this point, and the Reverend Archbishop was constantly besieged to confirm or deny the most outlandish and distasteful reports about what had occurred. At first His Eminence refused to speak to the press at all, but finally, by the time some scandal sheets were claiming that Nyarlathotep, the mad faceless god of Khem, had appeared on the altar bellowing *"Cthulhu fthagn!,"* the Archbishop issued a terse statement through his Press Secretary.

"Nothing untoward happened. His Eminence merely tripped on the altar rug, and any further discussion would be futile."

This merely fanned the flames of Rumor, of course.

One legend circulated even more than the others, perhaps because it appealed to prurient interest, or maybe just because it was the version given by a few people who had actually been in the Cathedral during Mass.

According to this yarn, a miraculous flying Rehnquist—just like the ones in the murals at Pompeii, except that it didn't have wings—had soared across the front of the church, barely missing His Eminence's high episcopal nose.

The judicious, of course, did not credit this wild rumor. They were all coming around, as the judicious usually do, to the view of the cynics. The Archbishop, they said, had been stewed to the gills.

His Eminence was no fool, however. After the first shock, he had begun his own investigation, aided by a few trusted deacons.

They found the slingshot, abandoned, on the floor of the first pew, to the right. That was the direction the Rehnquist had come from, and they all breathed a sigh of relief.

The Archbishop told them, then, the rumors *he* had heard about the incident of the Unistat Ambassador who had to be put on morphine after finding It, wrapped in pink ribbon, on a staircase.

"We are dealing with a deranged mind," His Eminence said, "but not with anything 'supernatural,' thank God."

They never found the Rehnquist, but as the Archbishop pointed out, "the perpetrator may have confederates."

Everybody tried to remember who had been sitting in the extreme right of the first pew. They carefully made up a list, including everybody's separate memories, half-memories, or pseudo-memories. The list looked like this:

> Lord and Lady Bugge
> Eve Gebloomenkraft and Admiral Hector
>   Horatio Fentwhistle, ret.
> the Hon. Guy Fawkeshunt, M.P. and
>   Eva Gebloomenkraft
> Ken Campbell and Eva Gebloomenkraft
> the Hon. Fission Chips, F.R.S. and
>   Eva Gebloomenkraft

"One name seems to stand out, doesn't it?" asked His Eminence.

"Eva Gebloomenkraft," said a deacon. "Isn't she that Jet Set millionairess who got into so much trouble in Unistat two years ago for putting laughing gas in the air-conditioning system at a meeting of the Joint Chiefs of Staff?"

GALACTIC ARCHIVES:

There are many legends about our magnificent Bard, but they are all murky, improbable, and contradictory. It is said that he was the leader of a Sex Cult and engaged in frenzied orgies every Wednesday. It is also said that he lived in faithful monogamy with a simple peasant woman from Galway whom he never married due to his distaste for Organized Religion and the primitive, brutal States of that period. And it is even claimed that he was the husband of Arlen Wilson, the sociologist and Futurist.

Other legends claim that our Bard was a shy, timid, scholarly person who never dared to sample any of the mind-altering drugs he discusses so casually. Contradictory rumors would have it that he consumed Gargantuan quantities of every possible kind of dope and never wrote except when he was, as the expression then was, "stoned out of his gourd."

He has been linked to the surviving witch cult, to voodoo, to the Rosicrucians, to the Libertarians, to the Discordians (some even claim he was a ringleader of the Discordian conspiracy against Law, Civilization, and Good Taste), even to the probably legendary Physics/Consciousness Research Group.

All that we know for sure is that the last Bard of Old Terra, as he is usually called, was born in Boston (probably descended from Mayflower Pilgrims) around 1930 or 1940 of the Old Calendar (*i.e.*, between 5930 and 5940 A.M.). He attended M.I.T., Harvard, and Cambridge University in England, but nobody knows what (if anything) he studied seriously. But we do know that he was recruited by the Communist Party and the C.I.A. in or about 1968 old style, to write a series of books that would destroy the moral fiber of the country and undermine the sanity of their readers.

(This was part of the Communist-C.I.A. plot to prevent anybody but themselves from finding out what was really going on. It is one of the charms of the Bard's style that he shows how this Double Cross system works, even while using it to befuddle and confuse his readers.)

What makes the archaic Bard of interest even today is that he had purposes of his own, unknown to his alleged employers in the Communist-C.I.A. Strange Loop Bureau. His books were intended to undermine *them*, as well as everybody else. He was planting the seeds of a new mythos, out of which emerged inevitably the galaxy of Immortal Superhumans in which we write this commentary.

COMING TO A HEAD

Technology is the art of causing change by Imagination and Will.

—Gen. E. A. Crowley,
Math in Theory and Practice

The sudden death of Bonny Benedict created waves of confusion and apprehension far beyond what ordinarily would have resulted from such a tragic accident.

The first one affected was Polly Esther Doubleknit, who called down from her executive office to the City Desk at once.

"What the hell happened to Bonny?" she demanded.

The City Editor spoke in a hoarse croak. "It seems to be what the TV news said, a heart attack." He was beginning to feel that he'd be the next victim, since his blood pressure seemed to be rising every minute.

"A heart attack?" Polly Esther was dumbfounded. "But what about the man?"

"He's being held, of course," the City Editor said. "But God knows what they'll charge him with—manslaughter, negligent homicide, who knows? There's never been a case like this before."

"They had better charge him with something," Polly Esther said crisply. "Or this paper will land on the D.A.'s office with all four feet. Do I make myself clear?"

Admiral Babbitt nearly jumped out of his skin when the news reached Washington.

113

"It's those Briggsing Bryanting faggots from Alexandria!" he screamed. "And they're gonna try to pin it on us!"

This was a defensive over-reaction caused by the fact that Old Iron Balls had been contemplating various ways of bringing about the demise of Ms. Benedict. But he distrusted Einstein and neuro-analysis—"Jewish egghead stuff" —and never realized that most of his mentations consisted of defensive over-reactions.

"I'll fix those Rehnquist-suckers," he said to an aide. "Get old de la Plume, and tell him I've got a big job for him."

This referred to Mr. Shemus de la Plume, Naval Intelligence's ace handwriting forger.

And so, within thirty-six hours, the *Washington Post* came into possession of a diary, allegedly written by John Disk, the man who had killed Bonny Benedict. The diary only *looked* cryptic at first glance. With a little study, anybody with at least two inches of forehead could figure out, from the abbreviations and clumsy codes used, that Disk had been an employee of the Central Intelligence Agency.

This was quite a shock to both Disk and the C.I.A., who had never had any connection with each other.

Actually, Disk had been raised in the True Holy Roman Catholic Church, a bizarre fascistoid splinter group which had broken with the Vatican during the reign of Pope Stephen of Dublin.

When Disk reached his adolescence in the early 1970s, however, strange things began to happen to him. At first he thought it was demons—he had seen *The Exorcist* and believed every bit of it—but his priest told him it was all because he kept Lourding himself.

Disk went to Confession every time he gave in to the temptation to Lourde-off, which was five times a week after he reached seventeen, and the priest kept telling him to use Self-Control and take cold showers. The priest also said that all the demons were in hell and Johnny should stop worrying about them.

The only people who believed in demonic possession, the priest said, were the benighted fanatics in the Orthodox Holy Roman Catholic Church.

Everybody in the True Holy Roman Catholic Church despised and hated the members of the Orthodox Holy Roman Catholic Church, which was another splinter group that had broken away from the Vatican during the reign of Pope Stephen. The members of the Orthodox Holy Roman Catholic Church hated them back, you can be sure. In fact, in the typical manner of splinter groups, they each hated the other more than they hated the common enemy, the heretics in the Vatican.

John Disk finally decided that what was wrong with him was not caused by demons and—since he was able to cut down on his Lourding-off to only twice a week after he passed twenty—it wasn't entirely caused by Sin, either.

He was being poisoned.

The reason he had cycles of agitation and elation, followed by cycles of anxiety and growing fear that everything was somehow unreal, was because he was eating an Impure diet.

The reason there were wars and rumors of wars, and revolutions and depressions, and pornography and lewd, sinful women in immodest clothing on every street was because all the food was full of toxic, mind-destroying chemicals.

The people responsible for this were the Triangular Commission, the Power Elite, the Elders of Zion, the Bavarian Illuminati, and the American Medical Association.

He had learned this by reading books on Organic Diet from bookstores run by the John Birch Society, the Natural Hygienists, the Purity of Ecology Party, and various other groups who were inclined to go through cycles of agitation, elation, anxiety, feelings of unreality, etc., and had realized this was caused by Impurity of Essence in their food.

John Disk read a great deal of this literature and changed his mind about twenty times before he finally decided which school of "correct nutrition" was really correct.

He decided Purity of Ecology was the group that really knew what the hell was going on. He believed every word in *Unsafe Wherever You Go* by P.O.E.'s founder, Furbish Lousewart.

By the age of twenty-three, Disk was a typical P.O.E. member. When not putting in his thirty hours a week working in their printing plant—where he received lodging and an Organic Diet in lieu of pay—he was out on the streets selling their newspaper, *Doom,* or giving away their four-page mini-pamphlets, which had titles like *Poison in Every Pot; Science: Satan's Plot against God and Man;* and *Jimmy Carter, Servant of the Jesuit-Zionist Conspiracy.*

P.O.E hated President Carter because he had defeated Furbish Lousewart in the 1980 election. But, with the typical logic of splinter groups, they did not hate Carter nearly as much as they hated Eve Hubbard, of the Libertarian Immortalist Party, who also got more votes than Lousewart, even though she came in third.

The P.O.E. people hated the Libertarian Immortalists for another reason, which was that the L.I.P. platform was blasphemous and unpatriotic.

Hubbard's slogan was "No more death and taxes."

She planned to end taxes by running the government like a profit-making corporation, terminating all interference in the internal affairs of other countries (thus allowing the military budget to be cut every year, instead of growing every year), and paying each citizen a dividend on the profits the Unistat Corporation earned through investing in space colonization to tap into the vast energy and resources of Free Space.

Hubbard planned to end death by investing the profits from space in longevity research, which the majority of scientists in the field were now convinced could lead to doubling or tripling human life-span in the first generation, and could lead to indefinite expansion thereafter.

The P.O.E. people realized that these proposals were scientific and rational.

They therefore regarded them as Satanic.

Most other people also rejected the Libertarian Immortalist program, but not on such superstitious grounds. Most people just said Hubbard was "too far-out" and Utopian.

Just about the only people who supported Hubbard were Dr. William S. Burroughs, the computer expert; Franklin Delano Roosevelt Stuart, the eccentric Black film director who was rumored to dabble in voodoo and Cabalistic magick; Simon Moon, the anarchist poet; and a disreputable psychologist named Alpert who had served twenty years in California's prisons for preaching weird ideas about re-imprinting the nervous system through chemical shocks.

And the three million outwardly conservative and inwardly Promethean engineers, doctors, and economists who had made up the original Libertarian Party back in the 1970s.

After three years in P.O.E., John Disk still had cycles of agitation and unreality; but the leaders of the cult assured him that it took at least that long for the poisons in his previous diet to leave his system totally. If he stayed on the correct P.O.E. diet, they insisted, he would become as serene as they were.

Still, things were getting to be more unreal more of the time. Disk looked in the mirror one morning, combing his hair, and seemed to see a middle-aged man looking out at him. It was only a flash, a single crack in the fabric of time, but it was unnerving. When the face turned back to his own—young, black-haired, pale—he wondered for a wild moment if he were truly a young man who had had a vision of himself twenty years older or a middle-aged man who was now having a hallucination of himself twenty years younger.

But that was only a short fugue, for in a moment he recognized that the face in the mirror was not his twenty-years-later, but rather a face that had adorned the cover of *Time* magazine a few months ago. It was the face of Dr. Francis Dashwood, president of Orgasm Research Inc., Commie pervert Satanist sinner who spent most of his time observing things that John would like to do but was afraid to do because of twenty years of conditioning by the True Holy Roman Catholic Church.

Which was bad enough, certainly, but not as bad as what was to come: voices at first so faint as to be barely perceptible, but slowly and insidiously growing louder, voices which were female and kept saying *You are George Dorn* and *Imagine you can see my Brownmillers through my sweater* and *The interpenetration of the universes has begun,* but mostly saying over and over *You are George Dorn.*

And there were occasions, only a second in external time but stretching to infinity in a multiple of new dimensions he found or created within, when the Sages would gather him into their Maybe-realm ("In addition to a *Yes* and a *No*, the universe contains a *Maybe*," was the password to pass the Lurker at the Threshold) and there would be Jesus saying "Is it not written, Ye are Gods?" and Emperor Norton saying "I just made myself Emperor of Unistat, Protector of Mexico, and King of the Jews," and Ped Xing saying "There are many universes and mindstates" and Beethoven singing the evolutionary scenario in eight cycles and Great Chtulhu's Starry Wisdom Band and Glorious Lucifer Son of the Morning who had never fallen because the message of the scriptures was written backward in a mirror and then Linda Lovelace would come in and start doing disgusting immoral things and he would be back, the splinter of eternity contracting to Euclidean 3D, standing on a street handing out *Poison in Every Pot* and wondering if he was losing his mind.

But the good parts of it were so good, Jesus and the weird but wise Emperor Norton and some of the Space Brothers, that he wished it would continue, if only it didn't keep turning into that sinful and disgusting business about Linda Lovelace; but he was beginning to figure it out; he was not the fool they thought him—not by a long shot. He knew that, now that the poisons in the food were beginning to wear off, They had started aiming an electronic Thought Control machine at his brain, so he did not pay attention no matter how many times the seductive female voice said YOU ARE GEORGE DORN YOU ARE GEORGE DORN YOU ARE GEORGE DORN.

So when he read that bitch, that Briggsing Bryanting whore for the Big Corporations and the Sex Educators and

Cattle Mutilators of the Satanist-Vatican-Zionist conspiracy, that lying tool of the Establishment, that contemptible Bonny Benedict claiming that Furbish Lousewart was a hypocrite and a meat-eater, claiming it when he knew it was not, could not be, true, damn her, the pig whore of the Jew-Jesuit money powers, as if a real Christian American like Furbish would pollute his body, the temple of God, with the flesh of a dead animal, the lying whore, he knew he would fix her and fix her good and proper, and show them all, the demonic jackal-headed lot of them with their laser beams flashing into his brain saying YOU ARE GEORGE DORN YOU ARE GEORGE DORN.

So he knew the perfect thing, the only way to express total contempt for the pig Establishment, the great lesson of the sages of the Clownological Counter-Culture, the attack that frightened, punished, and humiliated all at once and yet had to be endured as "only a joke," the bitch, that would fix her.

So he bought the pie, a Boston Cream special that was "rich and thick," according to the sign in the bakery, and waited for her in the morning outside the New York *News-Times-Post*-etc., and when the bitch, the lying whore, got out of her limousine, he was ready, he stepped forward, and he let her have it SMASH right in the face.

But then the old lady—my God, she looked like his mother, he realized—started choking and wheezing and fell down on the sidewalk and he knew. He knew even before the cop arrived from the corner, even before the crowd told the cop in great anger and outrage what had happened, even before the ambulance arrived, even before the doctor said, "She's gone."

And then the cop looked at him and he knew all the rest of it, the booking and the fingerprinting and the mug shot and then being alone in the cell all night with the voices saying YOU ARE GEORGE DORN.

Things were coming to a head.

Nathaniel F. X. Drest, secret chief of the Unistat Sector C.I.A., had felt uneasy for a long time. Since the death of President Carter, in fact. It wasn't just that the then-Vice

President, now-President, Hugh Crane, was right out of nowhere, a total unknown, not one of T.H.E.M.; similar situations had arisen a few times in the past, and the novice had easily been initiated into the secret science of Strange Loops and Mind Control, seduced—without the necessity of bribery, cajolery, or threats—into gladly becoming one of T.H.E.M. No: the unsettling thing was that Carter's death was unplanned, random, a surprise to everyone; it might even have been due to natural causes.

Yes: things were definitely and bodaciously coming to a head.

Nathaniel Drest had not lasted as secret chief of the C.I.A. for thirty years without acquiring great pragmatic savvy about the spooky side of predestination. "Once is happenstance, twice is coincidence, three times is enemy action," had been the motto of one of the great masters of Strange Loops, Ian Fleming himself; but Drest knew that what was *really* going on was far weirder than even Fleming could comprehend.

Behind the mild, professorial, bespectacled facade of Nathaniel Drest, offically listed as economics researcher in the budget reports, was the one man capable of serving as secret chief of the Unistat C.I.A. through thirty long years, while one dummy after another posed as the official head of the clandestine organization. Drest was a philosopher and a visionary; he had forged, from Machiavelli, Marx, Lenin, Mao, Mussolini, Nietzsche, Napoleon, William F. Buckley, Jr., and the Three Legendary Sages—Turing, Fleming, Wheatley—the coldly logical, existential, pragmatic strategy for eternal rule by himself and his friends in T.H.E.M., and total extermination and eradication of all possibility of rebellion by the rest of humanity.

He had been told once, by a sociobiologist, that he was a giant DNA robot, programmed to advance the growth and expansion of his gene-pool. He thought that was an amusing, although limited, view of what was going on; and he certainly had no interest in such evolutionary theories as justifications of what he did. He needed no justifications; that his goals were rationally desirable to him was all that was necessary or profitable to contemplate.

The world certainly deserved to be ruled by his gene-pool, by those White Anglo-Saxon Presbyterians and Episcopalians who had gone to Groton and Harvard, and occasionally there would be room for a bright boy from Yale, and this was so obvious that it needed no long-range evolutionary justifications. You just had to look around the world to see that no other gene-pool was smart enough, tough enough, and fundamentally liberal enough to do the job justly and wisely.

John Ruskin and Cecil Rhodes had seen the choice a century ago: a world ruled by one Anglo oligarchy on scientific and socialist principles, or a world of anarchy and chaos, with constant wars and revolutions. Of course, there had been some anarchy, chaos, wars, and revolutions since Drest had taken over, but that was due to surviving ideological poisons on the international system and would be cured when the planet had been on the correct, Drest-directed mental diet for a few more decades.

But things were coming to a head.

The damned Ruskies still obstinately clung to their obsolete Adam Smith economics, and much of the Islamic world was unruly and rebellious. But worst of all was the Discordian Society.

Drest knew all about the Discordian Society, or thought he did. He was convinced they were behind this latest attempt to discredit the Company with that forged diary linking them to the Bonny Benedict "Cream Pie" murder. He also believed that they were the secret organization behind all the lesser conspiracies that annoyed and sometimes frustrated him—the malignantly nihilistic Network that had Potter Stewarted his own computer and God knows how many other computers, the dupes in P.O.E. and the Libertarian Immortalist Party, the damned moralistic meddlesome Stephenites, Weather Underground, the traitors over at Naval Intelligence, the sinister Invisible Hand Society, the terroristic Morituri, and the damned Ruskies and Arabs.

Drest had first learned about the Discordian Society in a strange, obscene, subversive novel called *Illuminatus!* He was convinced it was all fiction, at first. But then he discovered that the alleged Bible of the Discordians, the perverse and paradoxical *Principia Discordia,* actually existed. When he put two men on the case, they soon reported that copies of the *Principia* could be found in many science-fiction and libertarian bookstores all over Unistat, and that it could be ordered through the mail from a company absurdly and disarmingly named Loompanics Unlimited in Dearborn, Michigan.

Of course, he wanted to believe that was all there was to it, just a small, oddball cult no more likely to influence events than the Libertarian Immortalists were. But then bit by bit the damning details accumulated. Emperor Joshua Norton, King of the Jews, was a Discordian saint, and Emperor Norton was also inexplicably becoming an "in" person. There was a play about Emperior Norton running in San Francisco, posters celebrating him for sale all over the country. The Discordian mantra "Fnord" was seen scrawled on walls more and more places, and on the pyramid on the back of the dollar bill. Characters in *Illuminatus!*, whom he had assumed were fictional, often appeared writing book or movie reviews for various magazines, and a check showed that they had been writing letters to the *Playboy Forum* and the Chicago newspapers since the early 1960s. Discordian cabals appeared in England, Germany, Japan, Australia, and the most unlikely places.

Drest had made a careful study of the Discordian philosophy and realized it was the kind of outlandish nonsense that would appeal to the kind of people who made all the trouble in history—brilliant, intellectual, slightly deranged dope fiends and oddball math-and-technology buffs. Many of the pioneer Discordians were computer programmers (he remembered that fact every time the Company's computer answered a simple program with GIVE ME A COOKIE, or THE GOVERNMENT SUCKS) and others had documented links with the Libertarian Immortalists, the LSD sub-culture, and groups as sinister as the witches and the anarchists.

The Discordians believed that God was a Crazy Woman. For the Woman part of it, they used the usual Taoist and Feminist arguments about the Creative Force being dark, female, subtle, fecund, and in every way opposite to Male Authoritarianism. For the Crazy part, they pointed to Pickering's Moon, which goes around backward, to rains of crabs and periwinkles and live snakes, to the paradoxes of quantum theory, and to the religious and political behavior of humanity itself, all of which, they claimed, demonstrated that the fabric of reality was a mosaic of chaos, confusion, deception, delusion, and Strange Loops.

And, Drest knew, they were most definitely linked with the Network. Although computer specialists only spoke of the Network in whispers, the Company had a detailed file on them. The Network was devoted to the long-suppressed, much persecuted, but persistent underground religion of cocaine founded by the eccentric physician Sigmund Freud. They devoutly believed in the literal truth of Freud's vision of the Superman. ("What is man? A bridge between the primate and the superman—a bridge over an abyss," Freud wrote in his *Diary of a Hope Fiend*.) To achieve the Superman, the Network was systematically frustrating every other group of conspirators on the planet by glitching the computers, and meanwhile systematically diverting funds from legitimate activities to subsidize dissident scientists engaged in research on immortality and higher intelligence. "Cocaine is a memory of the future" was the sick slogan of this misguided group of deranged intellectuals. "Our minds will function as ecstatically as on cocaine, *without the jitters,* once we achieve immortality and learn to reprogram our brains as efficiently as we reprogram our computers," they went on. "When we don't have to die and can constantly increase our *awareness of detail,"* they also said, "we will have no more problems, only adventures."

Naturally, every government in the world, even the near-anarchistic Free Market maniacs in Russia, had outlawed this bizarre cult.

An even more sinister Discordian front organization, according to Drest's coldly logical analysis of what was really going on, was the insidious Invisible Hand Society.

What was most devious about the Invisible Hand-ers was that they disdained secrecy and operated right out in the open, telling everybody what they were doing and why and what they hoped to accomplish. They had offices in all major cities and gave free courses in their politico-economic system just like the old Henry George schools at the turn of the century.

It was very hard for Drest to persuade the other eight Unknown Men who ruled the C.I.A. in other parts of the world that the Invisible Hand was the most dangerous sort of conspiracy.

"A conspiracy doesn't operate in the open," they kept reminding him. Sometimes they would tell him he was working too hard and should take a vacation.

"That's what's so subtle and devilish about it," Drest would explain, over and over. "Nobody can recognize a conspiracy that's out in the open. It's a kind of optical illusion that they're using to undermine us."

"But they don't believe we exist," he would be told.

"That's an over-simplification," he would insist. "They admit we exist and occupy space-time and so on. They just teach that all the titles we give ourselves are meaningless and all our acts are futile since the Invisible Hand controls everything, anyway."

The other eight would again suggest that Drest needed a vacation.

Things were coming to a head.

The first lesson given to people who signed up for the course of "Political-Economic Reality" at the Invisible Hand Society, Drest knew, concerned policemen and soldiers.

Two men in blue uniforms would appear on the stage, carrying guns.

"Blue uniforms are Real," the lecturer would say. "Guns are Real. Policemen are a social fiction."

Three men in brown uniforms would appear, carrying rifles.

"Brown uniforms are Real," the lecturer would say. "Rifles are Real. Soldiers are a social fiction."

And so it would go, all through the lecture. Pure mind-rot, and, thank God, most people found it all so absurd, and yet so frightening, that they never came back for any of the subsequent lectures.

But the people who did come back worried Drest; they

were the types he loathed and feared. Like Cassius, they had a lean and hungry look and they thought too much.

And they thought about the wrong things.

And now there was the matter of materializing-and-dematerializing Rehnquist, obviously a Discordian plot, in Drest's estimation. What other group could conceive it, much less organize and accomplish it? Fnord, indeed!

There had been the case of the Ambassador, who found it on a staircase; and the anti-pornography crusader, who encountered it, temporarily painted red, white, and blue, floating in a bowl of Fruit Punch; and that unspeakable incident involving His Eminence the Very Reverend Archbishop of Canterbury; and God knows how many other cases the Company had never heard about.

And President Crane was said to be far more of an oddball than anybody had realized, having strange groups for midnight meetings in the Oval Room, where incense was burned in profusion, and the Secret Service men claimed to hear strange chants that sounded, they said, like *"Yog-Sothoth Neblod Zin."*

Things were coming to a head.

THE OLD-TIME RELIGION

Magick is a mnemonic system of psychology to train
the Will and Imagination.

—Israel Regardie, *The Tree of Life*

Charles Windsor, Prince of Wales, was about to be crowned
King of England.

It was a sacred occasion for all British subjects, still
grieving for the Queen Mother, who had passed away so
suddenly. But in the midst of the mourning, there was
much excitement, since Charles would obviously make a
smashing king; he was bright, he was witty, he was good
looking, and he had sense enough not to meddle in politics.

There was one discordant voice in the crowd outside
Buckingham Palace waiting for the new king to return
from the coronation at Westminster Cathedral. This was a
plump, stately young Irishman who kept singing, off-key:

> O won't we have a merry time
> Drinking whiskey, beer, and wine
> On coronation
> Coronation day

Voices kept telling him to hush, but he would turn to
such spoilsports and say dramatically, "The sacred pint
alone is the lubrication of my Muse."

"Drunken ruffian," somebody muttered.

"Well, what if he is?" the Irishman said suavely. "He still
looks like a king, and is that not what really matters?"

"I wasn't calling the *king* a drunken ruffian," the voice
protested, too emotionally.

" 'ere, now, who's calling me bloody king a ruffian?" said
a soldier. "I'll knock the Potter Stewarting head off any

126

Potter Stewarting Bryanter that says a word against me Potter Stewarting king!"

"Hush," another chorus joined in.

"Don't hush me, you Bryanting sods!"

"It's overcome I am entirely," the Irishman said, "by the rolling eloquence of your lean, unlovely English. You were quoting Shakespeare, perchance?"

" 'ere, are you making sport of me, mate? I'll wring your Bryanting Potter Stewarting neck, so I will. . . ."

"Here he comes!" somebody shouted.

And other voices took up the cry: "The king! The king!"

Eva Gebloomenkraft, certainly the loveliest woman in the crowd, had been listening to all this with her own private amusement, but now she reached down and began to open her purse, a bit stealthily, perhaps, yet not quite stealthily enough, it seemed, for another hand closed abruptly over hers.

"Rumpole, C.I.D., Scotland Yard," said a voice, as a badge was flashed briefly. "I'm afraid you'll have to come along, Miss."

The Archbishop of Canterbury had shared his suspicions about Ms. Gebloomenkraft with the Yard, and they had been on the lookout for her all through coronation day.

But when they had her back in the interrogation room on Bow Street, there was no Rehnquist in her purse.

"I sold it," she said after an hour of interrogation. And, at their baffled expressions, she added, "It was becoming a bore. The joke was *wearing thin*. I needed something else to excite me."

"That's why you do it, then?" Inspector Rumpole asked. "For excitement?"

Eva raised weary eyes. "When you have so much money that you can literally hire anybody to do literally anything, life does become tedious," she said. "It requires some imagination, then, to restore zest to existence."

And all she had in her purse was a self-inflating balloon, which, when the cap was crushed, expanded to a sphere nearly twenty feet in diameter bearing the slogan, in huge psychedelic colors:

OVERALL THERE IS A SMELL OF FRIED ONIONS

When next recorded, the itinerant Rehnquist was in the possession of Lady Sybiline Greystoke, who had either purchased it directly from Ms. Gebloomenkraft or had acquired it from some go-between.

Lady Sybiline was an eccentric, even for the British nobility. She was so far to the right, politically, that she regarded the Magna Carta as dangerously radical. She was so High Church that she referred to Charles I as "Saint Charles the Martyr." She hunted lions, in Africa, and was a crack shot. She was also, secretly, president of the Sappho Society, the group of aristocratic Lesbians who had secretly governed England, behind the scenes, since their founder, Elizabeth I.

Lady Sybiline and her good and intimate friend, Lady Rose Potting-Shedde, evidently found great amusement, between them, with the Rehnquist, for they even took it with them when Lady Sybiline embarked, that summer, for her annual lion hunt in Kenya.

Their White Hunter on that expedition was a red-faced man named Robert Wilson, who, like Clem Cotex, knew he was living in a book.

Robert Wilson had discovered this when somebody showed him the book in question. It was called *Great Short Stories* and was by some Yank named Hemingway. And there he was, Robert Wilson, playing a featured role in the very first story, "The Short Happy Life of Francis Macomber."

It was a shock, at first, to see himself in a book, and it was a bit *thick* to find his drinking and his red face described so dispassionately. It was like seeing yourself on the telly, suddenly observing the-man-who-was-you from *outside*.

Then Wilson discovered that he was in *another* book, but changed in totally arbitrary ways that verged on surrealism. This book was a bit of tommyrot and damned filth called *The Universe Next Door*, and he was, in fact, both inside it and outside it, being both the author of it and a character in it.

Robert Wilson began to experience cycles of agitation, elation, anxiety, and a growing sense of unreality.

Then came Lady Sybiline and Lady Rose and that mysterious object they kept in a small box and kept joking about, obscurely, between themselves.

They called it Marlon Brando.

The river had pebbles at the bottom. They were shiny and small and the water rushed over them constantly and you could see clear to the other side if you had your glasses on and weren't too drunk. Robert Wilson stared at the pebbles, thinking they were like pearls, trying not to remember what had happened that morning.

"After all, it was a clean kill," Lady Sybiline said beside him. He wished she wouldn't talk. He wished she would go away and take Marlon Brando with her.

"The hills, in the distance," she said. "They look like white rhinoceri."

"They look like *white rhinoceri*," he said. "Jesus Christ."

"Don't talk that way."

"The bloody hills don't look at all like rhinoceri," he said. "They have no horns, for one thing. No exo-skeleton on the head. I never heard such a damned silly thing. They look like elephants, actually."

"Stop it," she said. "It wasn't that bad."

"It was bloody bad," he said. "Bloody awful bad."

"If it hadn't happened, would it be cute, then, for me to say the hills look like white rhinoceri?"

"It wouldn't be cute no matter what happened."

"Oh," she said. "It's like that."

"Yes," he said. "It's like that."

"Will you please please please stop repeating everything I say?"

The water kept running, always running, over the pebbles that were like pearls.

"It was bad," he said again. "Bloody awful bad."

"Are you always this rude to your clients?"

"Oh, it comes down to that," he said. "The hired help have to keep a polite tongue in their heads. You bloody English."

"You're English yourself," she said.

"I'm part Irish. I wish I were all Irish now."

"Really. You don't have to go on like this. Everybody is a little bit . . . eccentric."

That was the kind of whining excuse he despised. He knew then that he was going to be brutal. Somebody had to teach them.

"English literature," he said. "There is none in this century."

She cringed. He knew he had reached her.

"Stop it," she said.

"Everything worth reading is by Irishmen," he said. "Padraic Colum. Beckett. O'Casey."

"Stop it. Stop it."

"Behan. Bernard Shaw. O'Flaherty."

"Stop it. Stop it. Stop it."

"I'm stopping," he said. "I feel that I've said all this before, somewhere, already. But how could you do it?"

"It excites me," she said. "To have . . . Marlon . . . there . . . while I'm firing at a lion."

He shook his head. "You are a five-letter woman," he said wearily.

But then the Rehnquist mysteriously disappeared again, back in Nairobi, while Lady Sybiline and Lady Rose were staying at the glamorous new Mau Mau Hilton.

Lady Sybiline was furious, but frustrated. There was no way of asking the hotel to question its employees about the theft without describing the object that had been stolen, and that was, of course, potentially embarrassing.

But she and Lady Rose had lots of other exciting little games, and they soon forgot all about "Marlon Brando."

Especially after they bought a beautiful plastic-and-rubber imitation which they christened "David Bowie."

It wasn't really theft, of course; Indole Ringh was a pious and holy man who would never *steal* anything. It was his religious duty, as he conceived it, to remove the holy relic from the heathens and return it to its rightful homeland.

Indole Ringh was a brown, gnarled, perpetually smiling little man, the offspring of ten generations of very conservative Hindus who had never accepted English ideas or ideals.

He had, in fact, three personalities. One was just an ordinary Hindu nobleman who was always smiling. The second, when he was in *Samadhi,* was an awe-inspiring guru, no more human than a statue of Brahma. The third, when he was in *Dhyana,* was just the brightest, quickest, most curious monkey in the jungle.

He didn't believe in any of those personalities; he just watched them come and go, blandly indifferent.

Because he practiced hatha yoga, bhakti yoga, rajah yoga, and gnana yoga, and because he smoked a great deal of *bhang,* he was as *conscious of detail* as Clem Cotex or the late Pope Stephen. Because he believed the oldest *Vedas* were the important ones, he had no truck with modernistic notions of asceticism, British prudery, or heathen Missionary nonsense of any sort.

He was a devout worshipper of Shiva, god of sex, intoxication, death, and transformation. He believed that you couldn't come to your senses until you went out of your mind. He kept alive, within his own province, the ancient cult of Shiva-Kali, the divine couple whose embrace generated the whole play of existence.

And now, in Nairobi of all places, he had found, somehow in the possession of a heathen Englishwoman, the most sacred of all lost relics—the *Shivalingam* itself, the engine of the creative lightning.

131

So it was not theft at all; he was merely restoring the relic to the place where it belonged, to India.

In fact, he placed it on the altar in his own temple, and invited the whole province to come see it and marvel and know the power of the Divine Shiva, who possessed such a tool of creativity.

He was going to restore the old-time religion.

He made a speech to the assembled multitude on the first day the *Shivalingam* was displayed in the temple. He told them that the polarity of Shiva and Kali was the basic pulse of creation. He said the Chinese dimly discerned this in their *yin* and *yang* symbolism, and the heathen West in their concept of positively and negatively charged particles. He explained that the male-female polarity was the engine of creation, not just in the human and animal kingdoms, but in every aspect of nature. He said that *Samadhi* and *Dhyana* and normal consciousness were equally real, equally unreal, and equally pointless, but that if you contemplated this *Shivalingam* long enough it wouldn't matter whether you understood any of this or not.

He was so bombed on *bhang* that he kept going into *Samadhi* every few minutes during this, and the crowd, both his old disciples and newcomers, decided he was the wisest and holiest man in all India.

Old Ringh kept smiling and going into *Samadhi* and explaining that we are all bisexual immortals who inhabit many universes and mindstates, and the crowd kept cheering and getting higher on his vibes, and finally they all went into the temple and contemplated the *Shivalingam*, where Indole Ringh had placed it on the altar, facing the enormous carving of the sacred *yoni* of the Black Goddess, Kali, and under the faded photograph of the Wise Man from the West, General Crowley, who, even though an English heathen, had understood the Mysteries and had spent many hours, while smoking *bhang,* discussing with Ringh's father how, even in mathematics, the sacred *yoni* appeared in both the shape and the substance of 0, the void, while the *lingam* appeared in the shape and substance of 1, the creative lightning, and how, out of the union of the 0 and 1, all of the numbers of creation could be generated in binary notation.

And as everybody meditated on the miraculous return of

the *Shivalingam,* old Ringh remembered how General Crowley promised, when he had to return to the West, that he would use what he had learned in India to teach the whole world how the phallic spark of Imagination, represented by the 1 or *lingam,* generated everything out of absolute 0, the dark *yoni,* nothingness.

The
Third
Loop

Forget it, Jake. It's Chinatown.
  —Roman Polanski

OCCULT TECHNOLOGY

> Let me control a planet's oxygen supply and I don't care who makes the laws.
>
> —Great Cthulhu's Starry Wisdom Band

When Clem Cotex decided to program himself into the head space of the First Bank of Religiosophy, he sent five dollars to Bad Ass, Texas, for Dr. Horace Naismith's cassette tape, "The Occult Technology of Money and the Moneylords." By the time the tape arrived in the mail, Clem had been through so many *eigen*states, both as male and female, that he no longer wondered about "the stuff in the tomato juice" and was merely moderately surprised occasionally that most people were not as flexible in their thinking as he was. In fact, Clem had been a Scientologist, a solipsist, and a Logical Positivist, among other things, in the interim.

Filling a pipe with Alamout Black, the hashish of the Assassins, Clem lit up, toked deeply, and began playing the tape of "The Occult Technology of Money and the Moneylords."

"The Federal Reserve System—a private bank responsible to nobody, despite its name—creates money *out of nothing*," Naismith began in a pleasant Texas twang. Clem toked again and began to grok Naismith in his fullness. The tape played on and Clem toked again each time he felt the need to grok more deeply.

Naismith quoted Buckminster Fuller (the only Unistat President ever to resign from office) and Ezra Pound, the folk singer, and John Adams and Tom Edison and a lot of other people who had long ago been on Clem's list of folks who had probably been given some of the "stuff" in the tomato juice. All of these men, Naismith pointed out, had proposed money systems more efficient and more just than the present Federal Reserve System.

"There is no one money system that was ordained by God," Naismith said. "They were all invented by human beings and can be improved by human beings.

"Now, what is money?" Naismith asked. *"Money is information.* Ask any computer programmer about that, if you don't believe it. Money is a signal, a unit of pure information. It is as abstract as mathematics. Cattle served as money once. So did leather. So did the precious metals. They were commodity monies, because they were worth something in themselves. Modern paper money is pure information, worth absolutely zilch, except for the signals printed on it." Clem really began to get Naismith's perspective. He toked again, feeling the Big Idea behind the First Bank of Religiosophy.

"Money in the modern world," Naismith went on, "is no more than a promise to pay. If you look at the bills in your wallet right now, you'll see *what* they're promising to pay. They're promising to pay you more paper. They don't have to give you a gram of gold or silver or any real commodity. They'll just give you more paper if you want to trade in the paper you already have. Didn't that ever strike you as a *little bit funny?*

"Think of it this way," Naismith said, warming to his subject. "This is a corny old Sufi parable, but it might help you to get the picture."

The great Sufi sage Nasrudin, Naismith said, once invented a magic wand. Wishing to patent such a valuable device, Nasrudin waved the wand and created a patent office, which immediately appeared in 3D Technicolor.

Nasrudin then walked in and told the clerk, "I want to patent a magic wand."

"You can't do that," said the clerk. "There is no such thing as a magic wand."

Nasrudin immediately waved his wand again, and the patent office and the clerk both disappeared.

"Jesus and Ludwig Christ!" Clem Cotex cried. He jumped up and turned off the tape, totally At One with the doctrine of Religiosophy. "Money is information," he muttered, beginning to pace the room, stoned out of his gourd. "Holy snakes and ladders. 'Humanity is the symbol-

138

using class of life, and those who control symbols control us.' I read that in Korzybski aeons ago. *Information!*"

Clem sat down at his desk and spread out a large piece of paper. He drew an elaborate scroll around it and printed at the top: "COTEX RESERVE SYSTEM." He made it a cashier's check to the Treasury of Unistat for ten million dollars, to be repaid at the prime interest rate of fifteen percent. He then decorated another piece of paper, making it a Unistat National Bond, payable to the Cotex Reserve System for ten million dollars, thereby giving C.R.S. the credit to loan ten million to Unistat.

He then switched the pieces of paper around on the desk. Cotex Reserve seemed to be ten million dollars ahead, and yet Unistat owed *them* ten million plus fifteen percent interest per year.

["You can't do that. There is no such thing as a magic wand."]

Clem laughed hysterically. He remembered Simon Moon trying to explain Spencer Brown's *Laws of Form* to him: "To cross again is not to cross." Inflation, deflation, recession, depression: they were all like Nasrudin's patent office.

Clem knew he was in the state where synchronicities occur, so he went to his bookcase, picked a volume at random, and stuck his finger in, looking for the Message that would turn the whole experience into a full-scale Satori.

He was in *The Nature of the Physical World* by Sir Arthur Eddington, and the sentence he had found was:

> We have certain preconceived ideas about location in space which have come down to us from ape-like ancestors.

Clem Cotex laughed for nearly thirty minutes. The next time he met Blake Williams, he unleashed his Illumination in an aphorism that he was convinced would, for once, startle the seemingly unflappable anthropologist.

"Money is the Schrödinger's Cat of economics," Clem said, waiting for some sensational reaction.

"Oh," Williams said quietly, "you've noticed that, too?"

Dr. Horace Naismith had founded the First Bank of Religiosophy in Bad Ass, Texas, because he wanted to be sure nobody in the Establishment would take it seriously.

It was his plan to undermine the Federal Reserve System without their noticing what was happening.

Everything in Bad Ass was considered too absurd and repugnant for serious consideration. Bad Ass Township and the whole of Bad Ass County were a source of national embarrassment.

Bad Ass had been founded by descendants of the famous Jukes and Kallikak families, carriers of virulent idiocy genes, together with a few Snopeses who had been driven out of Mississippi for unnatural acts.

The Bad Ass School Board banned not only Evolution and Sex Education, but non-Euclidean geometry, the metric system, cultural anthropology, and all history texts written outside Texas.

Despite the President, the Supreme Court, Congress, the TV networks and Jack Anderson, the Bad Ass County Line still bore the traditional sign: DON'T LET THE SUN SET ON YOU IN BAD ASS, NIGGER. All roads leading to Bad Ass Township were littered with the decomposing bodies of murdered civil rights workers.

The only person from Bad Ass who ever managed to hold a job anywhere else became a drama critic in Seattle, Washington.

Everybody in Unistat was profoundly ashamed of Bad Ass and wished it were part of some other country. They never realized that, to the rest of the world, Unistat looked like Bad Ass County.

President Fuller, the man whose money ideas had inspired Dr. Naismith, was the only President in the history of Unistat to resign from office.

He had resigned only three months after taking office, and he did it on the radio. "I simply can't find any way to do anything socially useful here," he said with that innocent sincerity that had charmed the voters into electing him. "I listened to some well-meaning friends and ran for this office," Fuller went on, "and I now realize I was a perfect damned fool. The synergetic interlock or real time vectors in Universe cannot be augmented from here."

The people—and, even more, the other politicians—were outraged. They called Fuller a mugwump and wanted to punish him. Unfortunately, the only way to punish a politician is to refuse to vote for him, and Fuller was no longer a politician and refused to run for any office, so they had to be satisfied with just calling him a nut.

That was in the 1930s, and everybody forgot about Fuller until the 1960s, when it turned out that his hobby—odd geometries—had a lot of practical applications.

But still nobody took Fuller's money theories seriously, except Dr. Naismith, and Eve Hubbard, who had run for President in 1980 on the Libertarian Immortalist ticket ("An End to Death and Taxes!").

There was another President of Unistat who resigned, actually, but he "only" (as they say) existed in a novel. This was a science-fiction thriller set in a parallel universe and was called *Wigner's Friend*. It was about the worst possible President the author, a Harvard professor named Leary, could imagine.

The President in Leary's book, called Noxin, was a monster. He got the country into totally unnecessary wars without the consent, and sometimes even without the knowledge, of Congress. He lied all the time, compulsively, even when it wasn't necessary. He put wiretaps on everybody—*even on himself*. (Leary, a psychologist, claimed this bizarre fantasy, which smacked of satire, was possible, for a certain type of paranoid mind.) He used the F.B.I. and the I.R.S. to harass every citizen who resisted his tyranny. He not only took bribes, but even had a team of enforcers who extorted "campaign" money from corporations under threat of turning the I.R.S. on them. His political enemies all died in a series of strange assassinations that couldn't be explained. When Congress started investigating his crimes, he betrayed his own co-conspirators one by one.

Noxin even misappropriated government money to fix up his house, and cheated on his income tax.

The book was a runaway best seller, because it had a taut, suspenseful plot and because Unistaters could congratulate themselves on not being dumb enough to ever elect such a President.

Naismith, despite his Texas accent, was no imbecile; he had his finger on *part* of what was really going on.

The Federal Reserve did create money out of nothing. So did all the other banks.

The laws of Unistat allowed this, by permitting banks to issue loans up to as much as eight times the amount they had in deposits. Every time a bank made a loan on money they didn't actually have, they were *creating* money.

Most of the people who knew about this (aside from the bankers) went paranoid worrying about it. This was because they did not realize how much of their Reality was created in similarly occult ways.

The Federal Reserve made it possible for other banks to loan what they didn't have. The Fed *"guaranteed"* the credit of the banks.

The Fed was able to make this guarantee because it had lots of credit itself, in the form of government bonds.

The government bonds were good because they were guaranteed by loans from the Fed.

The loans from the Fed were guaranteed because the government gave them bonds.

And this was safe, because the bonds (remember) were guaranteed by the Fed.

That's why Clem Cotex laughed for half an hour when he finally figured out the Unistat economy.

The Communists had instituted this monetary policy because it made virtually all commerce dependent on money that didn't exist.

The Communists had abandoned pure Marxism in 1904 and were now following a system based partly on Marx and partly on traditional shamanism.

The whole Communist movement had secretly been taken over, in 1904, by General E. A. Crowley, the famous explorer. Crowley had learned a lot from the tribal shamans in the "backward" parts of the world he frequented. Chiefly, he had learned that the universe is created by the participation of its participants.

Franklin Delano Roosevelt was hand-picked by General Crowley to manage the Communist takeover of Unistat. Crowley picked Roosevelt chiefly because of his radio voice. The agreement was simple: Crowley would keep Roosevelt supplied with women—"That crip Casanova never gets enough," he was soon complaining—and Roosevelt, in turn, introduced Nasrudin's magic wand to political economy.

Even though many clear-sighted, patriotic citizens saw through Roosevelt and warned, repeatedly, that he was leading the country to Communism, the majority paid no heed to these voices of reason. They were charmed by Roosevelt's radio voice, as Crowley had predicted.

Actually, Roosevelt kept before him, every time he spoke on radio, a large sign with a wise saying attributed to the man who won the Bad Ass Hog Calling Contest in 1923. The sign said:

YOU'VE GOT TO HAVE APPEAL AS WELL AS POWER IN YOUR VOICE. YOU MUST CONVINCE THE SWINE THAT YOU HAVE SOMETHING FOR THEM.

Unfortunately, Roosevelt was assassinated by a disgruntled office-seeker in 1937.

The Communists found an equally loyal servant in 1948, however, in the famous General Douglas MacArthur, who was a military genius with one fatal flaw: he had an ego so large that only by contemplating the mathematical definition of infinity could anything so limitless be imagined.

MacArthur completed the Communization of Unistat in return for having his picture put on pennies, nickels, dimes, dollars, postage stamps, paintings in every public place, G.I.-issue condoms, the ceilings of barber shops, Mount Rushmore, the Sistine Chapel frescoes (advising God during the Creation), all government documents, the chief balloon in all Macy's parades, in place of the test pattern on TV screens, marriage licenses, dog licenses, and in various other places that he thought of from time to time.

A brave and patriotic senator, Joseph R. McCarthy, attempted to expose MacArthur's government, which was staffed entirely by card-carrying Communists. (The Communists carried cards because, with so many conspiracies going on at the time, it was the only way they could identify themselves to one another.) The senator was smeared by the press, censured by his colleagues, and hounded to an early grave.

"Ike" Eisenhower, a popular Western film star of the period, contributed to McCarthy's demise by making a national tour supporting the President.

"I don't know anything about politics or military strategy," old "Ike" would tell audiences, his face full of stupid sincerity. "But I know General MacArthur is a smart man and a tough man and can outfox the Commies every time."

Like almost everybody else, "Ike" thought the Communists had taken over Russia, not Unistat.

One of the most insidious things the C.I.A. Communists did when they took over Unistat was to change the Constitution.

The original Constitution, having been written by a group of intellectual libertines and Freemasons in the eighteenth century, included an amendment which declared:

> A self-regulated sex life being necessary to the happiness of a citizen, the right of the people to keep and enjoy pornography shall not be abridged.

This amendment had been suggested by Thomas Jefferson, who had over nine hundred Black concubines, and Benjamin Franklin, a member of the Hell Fire Club, which had the largest collection of erotic books and art in the Western world at that time.

The Communists changed the amendment to read:

A well-regulated militia being necessary to the security of a free state, the right of the citizens to keep and bear arms shall not be abridged.

All documents and textbooks were changed, so that nobody would be able to find out what the amendment had originally said. Then the Communists set up a front organization, the National Rifle Association, to encourage the wide usage of guns of all sorts, and to battle any attempt to control guns as "unconstitutional."

Thus, they guaranteed that the murder rate in Unistat would always be the highest in the world. This kept the citizens in perpetual anxiety about their safety both on the streets and in their homes. The citizens then tolerated the rapid growth of the Police State, which controlled almost everything, except the sale of guns, the chief cause of crime.

The Communists also widely distributed automobile bumper-stickers which said:

SUPPORT YOUR LOCAL POLICE

Although some libertarians and other soreheads tried to parody this (with bumper stickers that said SUPPORT YOUR LOCAL POLICE FOR A MORE EFFICIENT POLICE STATE), the majority were, as usual, too dumb to see how they were being snookered.

THE BACHS' BOX

> Magick is the art of causing change in consciousness
> by act of Will.
>
> —Dion Fortune, *Common-Sense Occultism*

The Wilhelm Friedemann Bach Society was in the same
downtown Washington building as the Warren Belch Society
and the Invisible Hand Society, but Clem Cotex never
thought much about them. He assumed, as did everybody
else who noticed the name on the building directory, that
the W. F. Bach Society was just a group of musicologists.

Nothing could have been further from the truth.

They were also trying to find out "what the hell is really
going on."

This odd fraternity had named themselves after W. F.
Bach not just for his music, which was superb, but for his
effrontery, which was even more superb. Wilhelm Friedemann Bach, one of the twenty children of Johann Sebastian
Bach, did not have the easy and immediate success of his
brothers, Johann Christian Bach and Carl Philipp Emanuel
Bach. In fact, because he was original and because he had to
compete with the other three Bachs (already well established in the esteem of music-lovers), Wilhelm Friedemann
was neglected for a long time and might have ended his
days in poverty and obscurity. But W. F. Bach was not the
sort of man to take defeat easily. He hit on a plan which
caused his music to be played everywhere, and made him
quite a bundle of Deutschmarks, even though people were
still saying he was the least important of the Bachs.

Wilhelm Friedemann had simply sold his compositions,
one by one, as newly discovered work by his father, J. S.
Bach.

Of course, there had been art forgers and music forgers
and even novel forgers both before and after W. F. Bach,
but he had raised the philosophical ante on the bothersome

question, "If a work of art cannot be distinguished from a masterpiece, is it not a masterpiece?" Or, in the vernacular, "How important is a Potter Stewarting *signature,* anyway?"

The original members of the W. F. Bach Society were people who had owned some magnificent Van Goghs back in the 1960s. Then one traumatic day, they did not own any Van Goghs at all. They owned El Mirs.

El Mir was the most talented painting forger of that time. His Van Goghs, Cézannes, and Modiglianis were totally indistinguishable from "the real thing," whatever that is. It was widely believed, after El Mir was exposed by another forger named Irving, that many masterpieces *still* hanging in museums were El Mir's work. Indeed, El Mir insisted on that, regarding it as the cream of the jest.

Some said that these El Mirs still hung in museums because the experts had not yet found any way to distinguish them from "real" art. Others said that the experts, once aware of El Mir's work, *could* distinguish it from Van Gogh's or Cézanne's or Modigliani's, but *would* not do so, because they had authenticated the fakes originally and did not want anybody to know that they had been fooled.

Blake Williams, Ph.D., had purchased a very fine El Mir, under the impression it was a Van Gogh, after the great success of his popularized book on primate psychology, *How to Tell Your Friends from the Apes.* Williams was then in the midst of his first phase of synthesizing General Semantics and Zen Buddhism, and he immediately recognized what was *really* going on when identifiable El Mirs were everywhere falling in value after the great Exposé.

It was a glitch, he decided.

He called together a small group of people who also owned identified El Mirs and begged them not to believe that they had been deceived.

"A signature," he told them earnestly, "is not an *economic Good* in itself, like gold or land or factories. It is only a *squiggle* given contextual meaning by social convention."

He went on like that for nearly an hour. He spoke of the differences between the map and the territory; between the spoken word ("a sonic wave in the atmosphere") and the *non-verbal thing* or *event* which the word merely designates; between the menu and the meal. He quoted Hume, Einstein, Korzybski, and Pope Stephen. He dragged in the latest

147

theories in perception psychology, Ethnomethodology, and McLuhan's version of media-message analysis.

He reminded them that Carlos Castaneda had studied Ethnomethodology with Garfinkle before studying shamanism with Don Juan Matus, and he assured them, as a professional anthropologist, that anyone who has the power to define reality for you has become a sorcerer, if you don't catch the bastard real quick.

By this time a lot of his audience was irritated and a little frightened—mutters of "He's just a damned crank" were heard from some corners of the room—but others were listening, enthralled.

Williams resorted to psycho-drama and Role Playing to get his point across. He said that he would pretend to be an extraterrestrial—"I wonder if it's *just* pretending," said an awed voice from the group who had followed this lecture with a sense of Illumination. Play-acting the extraterrestrial, Williams defied them to explain several things to him, rationally and logically, without assuming he had "intuitive" or *a priori* knowledge about what they took for granted.

He wanted to know, first, the difference between a dollar bill printed by the Unistat Treasury and a dollar bill printed by a gang of counterfeiters.

Everybody got excited, and most of them got angry, in the course of trying to make this distinction clear to the extraterrestrial, who was very literal and logical, and did not understand anything they took for granted until it was explained literally and logically.

By the time the extraterrestrial was willing to grant that there was an *agreed-upon* difference between the two bills *created by* social consensus, a few people had left, saying, "It's just an elaborate put-on."

But the others, who stuck it out, were next confronted with a dollar bill hung in a museum as "found" art. Williams, the extraterrestrial, wanted to know whether its value was the same as, greater than, or less than it had been before being hung in the museum.

More people lost their tempers in the course of this discussion.

But Williams persisted. Still playing extraterrestrial, he wanted to know if it made any difference if the dollar hung in the museum as "found" art had been printed by the Treasury or by the criminal gang.

After a few minutes of this topic, most of the people in the room were jumping up and down like the Ambassador who found the Rehnquist on the stairs.

Williams had no mercy. He next wanted them to explain the difference between any or all of the above and an *exact duplicate* of any or all of them painted by Roy Lichtenstein and exhibited as Pop Art.

After a half-hour more, he pointed out that they were arguing among themselves even more than they were attempting to explain these mysteries to him. He also mentioned, not too cruelly, that many of them had arrived at the state where they seemed to believe their definitions would become more convincing if they just repeated them at a louder decibel level.

Williams then gave up the extraterrestrial game and tried to restore order. He became droll and told them the old story of how Picasso, asked to identify the real Picassos in a group of possible fakes, had put one of his own canvases among the fraudulent group. "But," an art dealer among those present protested, "I saw you paint that one myself, Pablo."

"No matter," said the Great Man imperturbably, "I can fake a Picasso as well as anybody."

He reminded them that Andy Warhol kept a closet full of Campbell's soup cans, and gave autographed cans to people he liked so they could own "a genuine Warhol." He pointed out, after the laugh subsided, that neither extraterrestrials nor terrestrials could agree on the difference in value between a Treasury dollar signed by Warhol and thereby becoming "a genuine Warhol," a counterfeit dollar signed by Warhol for the purpose—giving "a genuine Warhol" to a friend, a Treasury dollar with Warhol's signature forged by El Mir, a Treasury dollar with Warhol's signature forged by an unknown criminal, and a counterfeit dollar with Warhol's signature forged by William S. Burroughs, the founder of Neo-Cubist painting.

He said that Ethnomethodologists knew that the border between the Real and the Unreal was not fixed, but just marked the last place where rival gangs of shamans had fought each other to a stalemate. He said the border had shifted after each major conceptual struggle, as national borders shift after military struggles. He defined everybody who attempted to define Reality, including himself, as a conscious or unconscious co-conspirator with some gang of shamans who are trying to impose their game on the rest of us.

He said that both the economics of art and the art of economics were determined by shamans, whether they knew themselves as shamans or not.

"*Crazy* as a *bedbug*," said the last man to quit the room.

The remainder were staring at Williams with devout awe. They felt that he had removed great murky shadows from their minds and brought them forward into the light.

Williams had made some Converts.

He settled back in an easy chair—he had been standing, in his Full Professor lecture-room style, through most of this—and got chatty and informal. He told them the little-known story of Pope Stephen's parable to the Spanish Cardinal who had told him that "seeking for the Real" was pointless since the Real is palpably right in front of our noses.

"Everybody knows," Pope Stephen had said, "that I studied singing and medicine before I decided to make the priesthood my life's work. What few know is that I also considered becoming a novelist. I often wonder, myself, if I ever abandoned that last ambition. Sometimes I feel like a novelist pretending to be Pope, to see what it's like. And sometimes I even think the whole Church is a very old novel which I've revised and modernized. And, my reverend brother in Christ, sometimes I even think that I'm not alone in this novel-writing business; I think that every man, woman, and child on this planet is writing a novel inside their heads, all day long, every day—editing, rewriting, touching things up, improving a page here and throwing a page out somewhere else. The only difference is that when I write a novel, it becomes an Encyclical, and is therefore Reality for millions of believers."

Williams now had five True Believers out of the thirty persons he had called together. The five, together with Williams, founded the W. F. Bach Society that night, and set out to impose their definition of Art on the rest of the world.

They began by finding and financing Orson Welles, an obese genius who might have been the world's greatest film director if he were only allowed to direct films.

Welles was not allowed to direct films because he had made the mistake, his first time out, of making a movie about Charles Foster Hearst, the richest and most powerful of the Communist clique who ruled Unistat. Welles changed the name, of course, and called his movie character William Randolph Kane, but few were deceived by this, and Hearst certainly wasn't.

The movie had a scene, at the beginning, in which a conservative banker said bluntly that "Kane" (Hearst) was a Communist. It went on to make a big mystery about the word "Rosebud," which referred to General Crowley's system of "Rosy Cross" Cabalistic magick which the Communists were using to make money out of nothing. It exposed, almost blatantly, how Unistat was actually governed.

Welles was blacklisted, and spent the rest of his life wandering around the world playing bit parts in films by other directors.

The W. F. Bach Society financed Welles in the making of his second film, *Art Is What You Can Get Away With,* which was a bold glorification of El Mir.

Next, the W. F. Bach cabal financed a new literary journal, *Passaic Review,* which they advertised so widely that everybody with any pretense to being an intellectual had to read it.

The *Passaic Review* heaped scorn and invective on the established literary idols of the time—Simon Moon, the neo-surrealist novelist; Gerald Ford, the "country-and-western" poet; Norman Mailer; Robert Heinlein; Tim Hildebrand; and so on. They also denounced all the alleged "greats" of the first part of the century, like H. P. Lovecraft, Henry James, T. S. Eliot, and Robert Putney Drake.

They established their own pantheon of "great" writers, which included William Butler Yeats (an obscure Irish schoolteacher nobody had ever heard of), Olaf Stapledon, Arthur Flegenheimer, and Jonathan Latimer.

After only two years of bombardment by the erudite and

authoritative-sounding articles in *Passaic Review*, most self-declared intellectuals were seriously comparing Yeats with Eliot and granting that some of Stapledon's novels were as good as anything by James or Drake.

All of this was an experiment, actually. Blake Williams had not believed *everything* he told the founders of the W. F. Bach Society. He was convinced that a *great deal* of what passes for Value was created, not by labor as the Marxists thought, nor by supply-and-demand as the Free Market economists claimed, but by what he as an anthropologist recognized as shamanism.

He was trying to find out how much Value, and hence how much Reality, was so created.

He believed that large hunks of experience could be altered by people who regarded themselves as shamans and considered anyone who opposed them to be rival shamans trying to sell an alternative Reality.

It was his plan to move the Bach group, slowly, from experimenting upon the economics of art to experimenting upon the art of economics.

He knew that Value was the Schrödinger's Cat in every equation.

THE MAD FISHMONGER

A ka dua
Tuf ur biu
Bi aa chefu
Dudu ner af an nuteru

—Ankh-f-na-Khonsu

"Gentlemen," Clem Cotex said smugly, "I believe I have identified the Mad Fishmonger."

The entire membership of the Warren Belch Society— all eight of them—were assembled in the tiny office, and a gasp of astonishment went up.

"Yes," Clem said emphatically, standing at the head of the table, under the portrait of Wigner's Friend, "I believe I have a positive *'make'* on the *'suspect,'* as Jack Webb would say."

Anthropologist Blake Williams, he of the monumental obsession upon Schrödinger's occasionally dead cat, spoke first. "Who?" he cried, almost in the tone of one who hears that the circle has, at last, been squared.

"Let me present the evidence," Cotex said with a solemnity that fit the occasion. He doused the lights and stepped to his slide-projector machine.

On the screen at the other end of the office appeared a well-known face.

"That's General Crowley, the discoverer of the North Pole!" exclaimed Professor Percy "Prime" Time.

"Yes," said Clem Cotex with deliberation. "General Edward A. Crowley, the best-known explorer and adventurer of the early decades of our century. The model of the English nobleman. The idol of young boys everywhere. General Crowley, indeed." He paused dramatically.

"Look at those eyes." Clem's voice suddenly had the

tone of Perry Mason addressing the court. "How would you describe those dark and brooding orbs, my friends?"

"Well," Dr. Williams said, "he has what I believe is called um a *piercing* gaze."

"Exactly," Cotex said. "A piercing gaze."

Another picture of General Crowley came on the screen. And another. And another.

"The same piercing gaze," Clem said pointedly, "year after year. No matter where he is when a photographer pops up—Africa, Mexico, the North Pole; it doesn't matter—always the same piercing gaze."

"Well ah aren't heroes *supposed* to have a piercing gaze?" Old Prime Time protested, wondering if this was just another of Clem's wild-goose chases.

"In a certain class of sensational fiction," Clem said tightly, "heroes have a piercing gaze. Sometimes the villains do, too—Fu Manchu for instance. But we are not living in that kind of novel," he went on, not bothering to tell them his opinion of what kind of novel they were living in. "In our reality, a piercing gaze means only one thing, and you all know what it is, gentlemen."

Another picture of General Crowley came on the screen, one in which he was much older than in the previous four photos; but he still had the same dark and deep—yes, piercing—gaze.

"These are the eyes," Clem said, "of a *hopeless slave of the hashish habit*. Now, as you all know, many English military men acquired a taste for the resin of the *Cannabis Indica* plant while in India, and were none the worse for it. Certainly, an occasional smoke of the hash is an enjoyable, even a mind-expanding, experience. I dare say most of you here have tried it, and I gladly admit that I have. But a sensible man keeps such diversions within certain bounds. Such a sane, sound man does not '*do a number*' [as our younger people call it] until evening, or at least until twilight. Well, maybe late afternoon occasionally. Perhaps in the morning *once in a while*. But not one stick of hash after another, day after day, year after year, for twenty, thirty, forty years! No: one who fits that description is a *slave* of the habit, a hashish robot, a man whose mind has lost contact with Reality [whatever that is] and wanders amid the phantasms of his own poisoned brain. A man, as the Irish say, whose mind has been taken away by the Wee People."

All gazed up at the photo of General Crowley, "the last of the Kipling heroes," as a journalist had called him, and Crowley gazed back at them, stony-eyed, impassive, enigmatic.

"Now, I have been studying all of General Crowley's wanderings," Clem went on. "He was, in fact, back in England during November of 1881. The crab and periwinkle prank would have been easy for a man of his wealth, if his mind had already acquired that strange quirk, that twist in the sensibility, which cannabis abusers refer to in their own argot as 'a spaced-out sense of humor.'

"In 1893, what do we find?" Clem continued. "General Crowley was visiting the Jersey shore, right here in Unistat, 'fishing and relaxing,' he says in his autobiography. And that very summer we see the first record of 'the Jersey Devil,' that fabulous monster that looked like a gorilla, jumped like a kangaroo, and glowed in the dark.

"I think we can discount later appearances of *the Jersey Devil*," Clem said argumentatively, "as the work of lesser pranksters, inspired by General Crowley's initial success.

"In 1904," Clem went on, "there was the famous werewolf scare in Northumberland. General Crowley was back in England that year. In 1905, we have the first major UFO flap in Spain. General Crowley was vacationing there. In 1908, gnomes and other Little Green Men were reported in Switzerland. General Crowley was there, allegedly only to climb mountains.

"And so it goes," Clem said bluntly, flicking the lights back on. "Over fifty-six percent of all the weird data collected by the conservative Forteans, by our own more imaginative group, and by all the UFO buffs, for the years 1860 to 1930—the years of General Crowley's life—correlate with the General's own movements. Even the Loch Ness Monster first began to appear after he bought Boleskine House, on the shore on Loch Ness.

"I think, gentlemen, that the conclusion is inescapable. General Edward A. Crowley, the mountaineer, the adventurer, the explorer, was a man unhinged by hashish abuse. He had become a compulsive, obsessive, sometimes sadistic practical joker. After all, I think the psychology of it is easy to understand, especially to those of us who, while not enslaved by the habit as he was, have had our own little adventures with the cannabis molecule. The world was becoming increasingly materialistic, bureaucratic, and—to a man like Crowley—*dull*. He set out to restore the Mysterious, the Magical, even the Frightening, to us. He was the last Romantic.

"I have no doubt of it," Clem concluded. "General Crowley was the Mad Fishmonger of Worcester."

"By George," Blake Williams said, "I think you've really got it."

There were murmurs of agreement. But then Professor Fred "Fidgets" Digits spoke up suddenly: "This opens a whole new can of worms," he said. "If General Crowley was—well, what he now appears to be, a common hoaxter—well, gentlemen, can we trust his reports on the North Pole expedition?"

"I fear not," Clem Cotex said. "That question came to me as soon as I began to realize Crowley's true character. We can't believe the North Pole story at all. It may just be another of his jokes. We may have been wrong for years, gentlemen.

"The earth may not be hollow, after all."

Down the hall, the Invisible Hand Society was having problems of its own.

A group of the more avant-garde members had become convinced of the existence of the Tooth Fairy and were trying to convert everybody else.

Naturally, Dr. Rauss Elysium did not like this. He felt it reduced the principles of the Invisible Hand Society to absurdity.

Dr. Rauss Elysium had summed up the entire science of economics in four propositions, to wit:

1. *Find out who profits from it.*

This was merely a restatement of the old Latin proverb —a favorite of Lenin's—*cui bono?*

2. *Groups never meet together except to conspire against other groups.*

This was a generalization of Adam Smith's more limited proposition: "Men of the same profession never meet together except to defraud the general public." Dr. Rauss Elysium had realized that it applies not just to merchants, but to groups of all sorts, including the governmental sector.

3. *Every system evolves and expands until it encroaches upon other systems.*

This was just a simplification of most of the discoveries of ecology and General Systems Theory.

4. *It all returns to equilibrium, eventually.*

This was based on a broad Evolutionary Perspective and was the basic faith of the Invisible Hand mystique. Dr. Rauss Elysium had merely recognized that the Invisible Hand, first noted by Adam Smith, operates everywhere. The Invisible Hand, Dr. Rauss Elysium claimed, does not merely function in a free market, as Smith had thought, but continues to control everything no matter how many conspiracies, in or out of government, attempt to frustrate it. Indeed, by including Propositions 2 and 3 inside the perspective of this Proposition 4, it was obvious—at least to him—that conspiracy, government interference, monopoly, and all other attempts to frustrate the Invisible Hand were themselves part of the intricate, complex working of the Invisible Hand itself.

He was an economic Taoist.

The Invisible Hand-ers were bitterly hated by the orthodox old Libertarians. The old Libertarians claimed that the Invisible Hand-ers had carried Adam Smith to the point of self-contradiction.

The Invisible Hand people, of course, denied that.

"We're not telling you *not* to oppose the government," Dr. Rauss Elysium always told them. "That's your genetic and evolutionary function; just as it's the government's function to oppose you."

"But," the Libertarians would protest, "if you don't join us, the government will evolve and expand indefinitely."

"Not so," Dr. Rauss Elysium would say, with supreme Faith. "It will only evolve and expand until it creates sufficient opposition. Your coalition is that sufficient opposition at this time and place. If it were not sufficient, there would be more of you."

Some Invisible Hand-ers, of course, eventually quit and returned to orthodox Libertarianism.

They said that, no matter how hard they looked, they couldn't see the Invisible Hand.

"You're not looking hard enough," Dr. Rauss Elysium told them. "You've got to notice *every little detail*."

Sometimes, he would point out, ironically, that many had abandoned Libertarianism to become socialists or other kinds of Statists because *they* couldn't see the Invisible Hand even in the Free Market of the nineteenth century.

All *they* could see, he said, were the conspiracies of the big capitalists to prevent free competition and to maintain their monopolies. *They*, the fools, had believed government intervention would stop this.

Government intervention was, to Dr. Rauss Elysium, just like the conspiracies of the corporations, merely another aspect of the Invisible Hand.

"It all coheres wonderfully," he never tired of repeating. "Just notice *all* the details."

Alas, the Tooth Fairy people were using all the same arguments. They said that if you couldn't see the Tooth Fairy, you weren't looking hard enough.

HONG KONG DONG

I gained nothing at all from Supreme Enlightenment,
and for that very reason it is called Supreme Enlightenment.

—Gotama Buddha

The fame of Indole Ringh's marvelous temple with the
legendary *Shivalingam* soon spread throughout India, and
pilgrims came from hundreds of miles away to look and
wonder.

The story even reached New York, where it caused
Blake Williams to write another scholarly article: "Phalli-
cism: Is the Old-Time Religion Making a Comeback?" He
compared the new mystique of Indole Ringh's *Shivalingam*
with the similar (although superficially very different) re-
actions in New York itself when Mary Margaret Wildeblood's Rehnquist was hanging on a plaque in her living
room, before it got stolen.

Even Williams, imaginative as he was, never guessed that
the same Rehnquist was involved in both cases.

The new cult did not last long, however, because some
miscreant crept into the temple one dark night and stole
the *Shivalingam*.

The multitudes were horrified, and even wrathful, when
the theft was discovered the following morning, but old Indole Ringh, smiling and spaced-out, made a little speech
that calmed them all.

"Miracles, like all other things," he said, "come out of
the Void for no reason and return to the Void for no rea-

son. Wait. Be patient. Pay attention to the little details. And see what comes out of the Void next."

Actually, the *Shivalingam* had not exactly returned to the Void, but had merely been transported to Hong Kong.

The King Kong Dong had been brought to Hong Kong by an unsavory person named Chi Ken Teriyaki, who was wanted by the authorities in Japan for selling "American" cigarettes made in Taiwan, diluted shark-repellent, stocks and bonds in a tapioca mine in Nutley, New Jersey, cocaine cut with Clorox, forged copies of the now high-priced El Mir forgeries of Van Gogh, and similarly dubious merchandise. Chi Ken, a half-Chinese, half-Japanese hoodlum, had originally worked for the infamous Fu Manchu and was later part of the notorious Casper Gutman mob in Istanbul. Fallen on lean days, he now eked out a bare living as a police informer in Hong Kong and part-time actor in underground Okinawan porn movies.

Chi Ken purloined the ithyphallic eidolon from Indole Ringh's temple of Shiva because he knew of a fabulously rich man in Hong Kong who happened to be looking for just such an item.

Hong Kong at that time, like most of the Orient, was haunted by the specter of the "boat people," refugees from Unistat who had crossed the Pacific in hopes of a better life. There was no nation in the East willing to accept more than a handful of these pitiful people, and most of them just drifted from harbor to harbor, slowly starving, and hoping for acceptance somewhere.

These desperate people were fleeing the appalling conditions that prevailed in Unistat since Furbish Lousewart became President in 1980.

The man Chi Ken Teriyaki was going to see was named Wing Chee, and he was a deep, dense, secretive person, even more inscrutable than the average Chinese businessman.

Wing Chee had been an athlete in his youth and had even toured Unistat once, performing amazing karate feats in a carnival. His missing right eye (the black patch made him even more inscrutable) was said to be due to an unfortunate incident that had occurred when the carnival was in Bad Ass, Texas, and he tried to use the white washroom at a gas station.

Mr. Wing had returned to China, and thence to Hong Kong, and had grown fat and rich by prosecuting what he considered a judicious and appropriate campaign of revenge against Unistat. He mass-manufactured fake T'ang dynasty art, to swindle the Unistat millionaires. He was the highest-paid informant for the C.I.A.'s Far East office, and, due to his knowledge of Unistat, always turned in information that confirmed the paranoid fantasies of his employers but had no connection with what was actually going on anywhere. Through a series of fronts, he had taken over organized crime in Unistat and arranged that everybody would blame it on the Sicilians.

He was currently engaged in smuggling as many as one thousand of the "boat people" a month into Hong Kong, where he put them to work in his factories and paid them three cents a day.

Wing Chee, at eighty-seven, was a philosopher and a man of balance. His life-style always tempered severity with mercy, larceny with generosity, sensuality with meditation. He always tried to be as just a man as was compatible with being a rich and comfortable man.

If one of the employees in his factories showed initiative or talent, Wing Chee noticed, and that man or woman was quickly promoted to a position of responsibility and solvency. He was no xenophobe; this policy applied even to Japanese, Hindus, and the wretched Unistat refugees.

Mr. Wing lived on Peach Blossom Street and had a magnificent view of all of Hong Kong and the harbor. He felt that the view was making him more philosophical every year. Each evening, after his twilight meditation period, he would sit at his window, smoking a long black Italian cigar, and look down at the teeming human hive below him, thinking that every person down there was the center of a whole universe, just like himself.

He had learned total detachment from all his own emotions in one split-second, the day the White cops in Bad Ass had knocked his eye out while arresting him. He had known, in that second, that he could kill them all—no man in the world knew more of aikido, judo, kung fu, and karate than Wing Chee in his youth—but he knew what would happen after that, if he did it. He looked at his own rage, understood suddenly in a mini-Satori that this was a mechanical-chemical process in his body, and became the clear mind that watched the rage instead of the emotional mind that experienced it. All of the more mystical and obscure things his martial arts teachers had tried to teach him abruptly made sense. He was never the same man again.

So he would sit, in the early evenings, smoking his foul Italian cigars (a taste acquired from a business associate named Celine) and look down at Hong Kong and its myriad of robots, each driven by mechanical and chemical reflexes, each believing itself the center of the universe. And then he would laugh softly at his own sense of superiority, because he knew that he was also controlled by chemical chains that determined what he could and could not think. Only in very deep meditation, and only a few times, had he broken those chains and seen—briefly! how briefly!—what the hell was really going on, outside of his own mental card-index system.

But Wing Chee always came out of those high moments giggling foolishly, like a mental defective, or weeping quietly at the stupidity of himself and the rest of humanity, or simply dazed, like a man who opens the door to his own bedroom and finds himself lost in one of the craters of the moon.

On September 23, 1986, Wing Chee had two important visitors in his office.

The first was the robot who used the name Frank Sullivan. Wing Chee gave him a neatly typed report full of nonsense and mythology about Far Eastern affairs, which Sullivan would dutifully turn in to Nathaniel Drest at

C.I.A. headquarters in Alexandria; Drest would worry even more that the Discordians were taking over the world.

Sullivan gave Wing Chee a cashier's check for twenty thousand dollars, from U.S. Silicon and Sherbet, which was the C.I.A. front for payments made to the Far East sector. Sullivan also gave Wing Chee a check for one hundred thousand dollars, from Universal Synergetics Inc., which was the front for the heroin industry's payments to the Far East. Wing Chee gave Sullivan a small ticket, which would pass him into a warehouse where the bricks of pure opium would be turned over to him, to be transported via the Corsican Mafia to France, where it would be refined into heroin, shipped to New York, and seized by a cop named Popeye Doyle. The last part of the process, the intrusive Doyle, was not part of the plan, but happened, anyway, to one shipment in two hundred, and was part of the overhead.

Wing Chee liked pseudo-Sullivan, even though he knew the robot was not human. It was comforting to talk to an organism that possessed no emotions and saw everything clearly, down to every last tiny little detail.

That ability to observe objectively was what made the robot such a superior Intelligence Agent, Wing Chee surmised.

The robot had, in fact, once been a human being.

Then he joined the U.S. Marine Corps, where they sent him to Boot Camp and brainwashed him.

The marines, of course, did not know that what they did was brainwashing. They called it "turning a civilian into a marine." It consisted of breaking down every imprint and reflex in the brain, through stress, shock, and constant humiliation, and then imposing a new set of imprints and reflexes. All military organizations did it, and none of them knew it was brainwashing.

The semi-robotized, semi-human product of Boot Camp was then among the lucky twenty—or the unlucky twenty—to be chosen for special training by Naval Intelligence.

He was then brainwashed a second time. The technicians who worked on him this time were more sophisticated than the Drill Instructors in Boot Camp, but they still didn't like to call their work brainwashing. "Brainwashing," they all felt, was what the enemy did. What they did was "turn a dumb marine into a trained Intelligence agent."

They used stress, shock, indoctrination, hypnosis, LSD, and conditioning.

The resulting humanoid subsequently defected to Russia and was brainwashed a third time by the K.G.B. What came up, of course, was a Strange Loop: under ordinary hypnosis, he appeared to be what he claimed to be, a sincere convert to the Russian way of life; under mind-drugs and deeper hypnosis, he was a Naval Intelligence agent, as the K.G.B. suspected all along. They proceeded to brainwash him a fourth and fifth time, and he returned to Unistat to be debriefed and to serve as a sleeper agent for the K.G.B.

Naval Intelligence then reprogrammed him again, digging out the third level that the K.G.B. couldn't reach. This level operated like a Trapdoor Code in a computer, and was inaccessible to anyone, including the programmed agent himself, except for those who knew the triggering word, which happened to be "Fishmonger," because the Naval Intelligence psychologist who had devised this system was a Charles Fort fan.

Naval Intelligence now had a man, or what had once been a man, who was accepted totally by K.G.B. as one of their very own, and who even defined himself that way *to himself,* but who was, at the word "Fishmonger," an Objective Observer for Naval Intelligence. He was exactly the twenty-third to have gone through this Strange Loop.

At this point the time-dwarfs from Zeta Reticuli got him with a classic Close Encounter of the Third Kind. All he ever remembered, and all he could tell either the K.G.B. or Naval Intelligence, was that a flashing light had come out of the sky, he had been paralyzed, and then it was three days later and he was in another city. Everybody assumed this was some brain spasm caused by the amount of imprinting and re-imprinting he had gone through.

But the Reticulans counted him as number 137 of their agents on Earth.

All his I.D. identified him as Frank Sullivan, of Dublin, Ireland, and even when he went through the brainwashing, or "basic training," as it was called, in the Provisional Irish Republican Army, that *cover* stood up.

Neither he nor anyone else remembered, by 1987, that he had been born Lee Harvey Oswald.

Wing Chee's second visitor that day was the unsavory Chi Ken Teriyaki, and their business was of a sort that most of the world would have regarded as extremely grisly and perverse.

But when Teriyaki left, two thousand dollars richer, Wing Chee was an extremely happy man. He canceled all his appointments for the day, summoned his chauffeur, and sped like a bullet to the home of Ying Kaw Foy, the youngest, the loveliest, and the most beloved of his three mistresses.

"My youth has been restored," he told the startled young lady. "I feel like a mere lad of forty-eight again! A whole new life is opening for us."

There was no mistaking the glint in the old man's eye. "The ginseng worked?" Ms. Ying asked, delighted.

"Well, not quite," old Wing said carefully. "But this is almost as good. We can nearly Potter Stewart again."

"My little old darling," Ms. Ying said. "I have told you that it gives me great pleasure to Briggs you, no matter how long it takes. And you Briggs me most deliciously and perfectly. And we are happy so, are we not? And what do you mean by these strange words? How on earth does one *nearly* Potter Stewart?"

Wing opened his package and showed her.

"Good grief!" Ms. Ying cried. "You've had your agents mutilate Mick Jagger!" But then her eyes misted over. "You'd do anything to please me, wouldn't you? You little old *darling*."

THE SYMPOSIUM

We will have immortality before the turn of the century.

—Dr. Benjamin Frank, 1978

When Simon Moon joined the Warren Belch Society, the effect was not additive, but synergetic. Simon the Walking Glitch added to minds like those of Clem Cotex and Blake Williams could only result in what a nineteenth-century philosopher had foreseen as "the transvaluation of all values." A new cosmology, a new theology, a new eschatology, and even a new theory about the metaphysics of *Krazy Kat* emerged.

Unfortunately, they all got so stoned that they could never remember afterward exactly what they had decided. It was like the legendary Cthulhucon of 1978 or 1979, which was supposed to have taken place in Arkham, Massachusetts. Every science-fiction fan in the country was alleged to have been there, and if they denied it, they were told that "the hash was so good almost everybody forgot everything that happened." Nobody ever knew, for sure, if Cthulhucon had itself happened, or if it was just a hoax, a legend created by a minority to perplex and annoy the majority.

Fortunately, or unfortunately, the Belchers all got together a week later, to try to reconstruct their great discoveries.

"I think," Simon Moon ventured, "that we all sort of agreed that Tristan Tzara, writing poems by picking words out of a hat, created the whole modern esthetic, while Claude Shannon, generating Information Theory by picking

166

words out of a hat, generated the correct approach to quantum mechanics."

"Jesus," Blake Williams protested, "did I agree to *that?* What the hell were we smoking, anyway?"

"Wait a minute," Cotex said. "Simon has *something,* dammit! Didn't we discover that there is a second flaw of thermodynamics as well as a second law?"

"I think," Percy "Prime" Time said, "that we were discussing *Deep Mongolian Steinem-Job* and that got us into the subject of unusual combinations and permutations."

"Yes yes, by God!" Williams exclaimed. "We realized that genius consists of looking for unusual combinations. Alekhine checkmates with a pawn, while his opponent is worrying about his queen. Beethoven proceeds from the third movement to the fourth without the usual break . . ."

"And Shakespeare makes a powerful iambic pentameter line, one of his most tragic, out of the same word repeated five times," Simon interjected.

"And Picasso constructs a bull's head, and a mighty sinister one," Father Starhawk said, "from the handlebars and seat of a bicycle."

"And so," Simon Moon cried triumphantly, "the unusual combination is the key to creative genius, and Tzara did find a mechanical analog to it in picking words from a hat at random. And Shannon formulated it mathematically when he realized that information is nothing but unexpected combinations—negative entropy in thermodynamics!"

"Jesus, run that by me again," Prime Time said faintly.

But Blake Williams had the ideational ball and was running with it. "So Dada Art and cybernetics are both ways of playing games with thermodynamics, with the laws of probability," he said. "By God, I'm becoming a mystic. The only way the universe or universes can survive is by continuous acts of creativity—unusual combinations—on some level or another. Schrödinger was right all along: life feeds on negative entropy. The mind feeds on negative entropy. The best favor you can do for anybody is to shock them, and no wonder the Zen Masters hit you with a stick when you least expect it; by God, any shock that's severe enough is a new imprint. . . ."

"Imprint?" Professor Fred "Fidgets" Digits asked wanly.

"A hard-wired circuit in the nervous system," Williams

said. "Imprints are created by shock. The birth process it-self is the first shock and makes the first imprint. Haven't you ever read ethology?"

"You mean like a gosling imprints its mother, and if the mother isn't right there it imprints some other white, round object like a Ping-Pong ball?" Digits said. "Yeah, I read that in Konrad Lorenz. Didn't he win the Nobel for it?"

"Well," Williams said, "I've been wondering for years about the Hollandaise Sauce mystery—the people who were poisoned by contaminated Hollandaise once and then had a toxic reaction whenever they tried to eat Hollandaise. That's an imprint, I decided. Being poisoned is uh you must admit, a shock."

"Oh, wow," Simon Moon said. "That's like Dashiell Hammett's story about the guy who almost got killed by a falling girder. All his imprints got extinguished. He just wandered off, forgetting his wife, his family, his job, and everything, looking for another Reality he could hook on to."

"Yes, yes," Williams said. "You're getting it. It happens to shipwrecked sailors and other people in isolation for long periods, too. The imprints fade and whatever comes along makes a new imprint. It happens in Free Fall; that's why all the astronauts come back mutated. And it happens at the first Millett, too."

"Far Potter Stewarting out," Simon said. "You mean, I dig red-haired women because my first Millett was with a red-haired girl in high school?"

"You've *got* it," Williams said. "If it had been a young um lady of color, you'd be one of those cats who only like to swing with Black chicks."

"If it had been a boy," Simon said, "I'd be Gay!"

"That's it, that's it!" Clem Cotex cried. "If the Finkel-stein multi-worlds model in quantum mechanics is true, there *are* universes in which you did take those imprints."

"Yeah," Simon said. "I can see myself hanging around Gay bars in one universe, chasing Black foxy ladies in an-other. . . . My God, it's probably true on the semantic circuits, too. There might be a universe where I imprinted mathematics instead of words. I might be a physicist or a computer specialist over there instead of a novelist. . . ."

"And," Father Starhawk said solemnly, "there might be

a universe where, with a different set of emotional and semantic imprints, I might be a professional criminal, a jewel thief, or something."

There was a pause, while everybody considered what they had been saying.

"This is all rather speculative," Fred Digits said finally. "We're being carried away by our own rhetoric, I suspect."

"Um another thing," Father Starhawk said. "People seem to be changing rather abruptly and in strange, unexpected ways lately. Those negative entropy connections and unusual combinations, you know? I mean, people who've been Straight all their lives and suddenly they're Gay or Bi or something. And conservatives suddenly becoming liberals, as if all the semantic imprints are fading everywhere. Stable people schizzing out. Emotional neurotics suddenly becoming mature. It can't all be the shocks of accelerating social change, can it?"

Blake Williams beamed. "That's the question I've been asking myself for months," he said, "and I think I have the answer. Gentlemen, all the so-called recreational drugs that have come into wide use in the last few decades may be chemical shock devices. I think people are bleaching out their old imprints, and accidentally making new ones, when they think they're just getting high and having fun."

"Wait a *minute,*" Simon said. "Isn't there a guy in prison in California for the last twenty-seven years or so for saying that? Some psychiatrist named Sid Cohen or something?"

"Never heard of him," said Prime Time. "Besides, we don't put people in jail in this country for their ideas."

"Well, anyway," Simon said, "even if all these new imprints made with dope are more or less accidental and the people doing it don't know what they're doing actually, it sure has stirred up a lot of the creative energy we were talking about. New combinations—bizarre, unthinkable, taboo combinations—are forming in brains all over the world every few minutes. Maybe that's why the Libertarian Immortalist Party could come out of nowhere and win the election by a landslide. 'No more death and taxes.' My God, who would have thought of it, twenty years ago?"

Father Starhawk grinned. "Who would have thought a

Black woman like Eve Hubbard could be President on *any* ticket?" he asked.

After the meeting broke up, Clem Cotex hung around the office a while, bringing the files up to date, dusting the Venetian blinds, wondering why Dr. Hugh Crane, the most brilliant mind in the whole society, had been so quiet during this meeting, and also speculating idly about how the novel he was in was going to end.

There was a knock on the door.

"Come," said Clem. He had picked that up from his hero, Captain (now Admiral) James T. Kirk, and he thought it was much classier than "Come in."

A small, brown, charismatic Puerto Rican opened the door. "Hugo de Naranja," he said, introducing himself Continental-fashion.

"Clem Cotex," Clem said. "What can I do for you?"

"You investigate the *eem*possible, not so?"

"Have a seat," Clem said. "We investigate the Real," he added, "especially those parts that the narrow-minded and mentally constipated regard as impossible, yes."

Hugo sat down. "I am initiate," he said, "in *Santaria*. Also in *Voudon*. I am poet and shaman. I am also—how you say?—goan bananas over one *mee*stery all my training in *Magicko* cannot explain. I theenk the Novelist play a treek on me."

"Oh, ah," Clem said thoughtfully, "you're aware that we're living in a novel?"

"Oh, *sí*, is it not obvious?" Hugo smiled, one weathered quantum-jumper to another. "You look at the leetle details, you see much treekery, no?"

"Remind me to study this *Santaria* sometime," Clem said. "It's given you a broad perspective, I can see. Now, what's your problem?"

"Poetry, it earns no much the *dinero*," Hugo said. "I work nights as watchman, to keep body and soul together. You know? So one night in the warehouse I see thees cat— thees son-of-a-beetch of a cat—and it is there and it is not there. You know?"

"Oh, certainly," Clem said. "You should take Blake Williams' course on quantum physics and neuro-psychology."

"Son-of-a-beetch," Hugo said. "I took that course, but I no pay attention much. Just to get the credit to get the degree. You know? I mees something important?"

"Every modern poet and shaman should know quantum physics," Clem said sternly. "Specialization is old-fashioned. You see, Señor de Naranja, what you encountered was Schrödinger's Cat, and Schrödinger's Cat is only in this novel part of the time."

NO LIMITS ALLOWED

No limits allowed, no limits exist.

—John Lilly, *The Center of the Cyclone*

"The man from the F.B.I. is here again," Ms. Karrig said, "with a man from the District Attorney's office."

Dr. Dashwood breathed deeply. "Send . . . them . . . in," he said as calmly as he could, clicking off the intercom.

He stared at the door for one frozen moment, still breathing deeply, relaxing every muscle; and then the door opened, and the two men came in.

I could jump out the window, Dashwood thought. But then he controlled himself.

He recognized Tobias Knight at once, but the man from the D.A.'s office—who looked like a young Lincoln, or Henry Fonda playing young Lincoln—was a stranger.

"Dr. Dashwood," Knight said cordially, "this is Cotton DeAct, from the District Attorney's office."

"Named after Cotton Mather?" Dashwood asked inanely.

"Named after Cotton Hawes, the detective," DeAct said, looking embarrassed. "My mother was a great mystery-story fan."

"Oh," Dashwood said. There didn't seem to be any other appropriate comment.

There was a pause, and Dashwood noticed that Tobias Knight looked a bit embarrassed, also.

"Well, gentlemen," he said heartily, "what can I do for you?"

"Hrrrmph!" DeAct cleared his throat. "Dr. Dashwood," he said formally, "there are two detectives from the Vice Squad waiting outside. They have a warrant for your arrest um for violating Section 666 of the revised criminal code ah Bestiality." He was actually blushing.

172

"I see," Dashwood said. He realized that his breath had become shallow and his muscles were tensing; with an effort, he relaxed. "I've known this day might come," he said with icy calm. "Why don't they just come in and arrest me, then?"

DeAct took a chair; Knight remained standing—between Dashwood and the window, although not being conspicuous about how he got himself there.

"Well ah," DeAct said, lighting a cigarette nervously. "You are ah um an International Celebrity in a sense um people say Freud Kinsey Masters Johnson and Dashwood almost in one breath you might say. Ah there are questions of Scientific Freedom at stake here. Ah there is the matter of our national image ah we don't want you to be called the American Sakharov or anything like that ha-ha right?"

"Do you mean," Dashwood cried, "you might offer me a deal?"

"Well, I can't speak with any authority on that," DeAct said quickly. "What we have in mind is having you ah fill us in on the background details."

"You mean you want me to inform on my colleagues," Dashwood said, not quite making a question of it.

"No no nothing like that," DeAct said. "It's hardly necessary, anyway. We know who they are and where they are, all sixty-seven of them." He noted Dashwood's reaction. "Yes," he went on, "there is very little we *don't* know about Project Pan, as you called it."

"Oh, Burger," Knight said suddenly. "Let's stop fiddle-Stewarting around. We've been on this investigation for over a year, Dashwood. We know that you and your friend Blake Williams somehow or other induced sixty-seven top scientific brains to get embroiled with you in this, this, this . . ." He blanched, and then went on brutally: "We know you've been *Lourding animals,* dammit! Lourding *donkeys* and Lourding *goats* and Lourding God-knows-what-else—whatever your Rehnquists would fit into, evidently. *Jesus Christ,*" he added. "I never heard of such a thing."

"That's enough, Tobias," DeAct said sharply. "You see our problem, Dr. Dashwood. Even in this age of sexual permissiveness and Free Scientific Inquiry, you seem to have crossed a line into very ah controversial territory, as well as being in violation of Section 666, the Bestiality law.

What we want to know is"—he paused for a deep breath—
"*why* did you do it, Doctor? And how in *hell* did you get so
many important people involved?"

"My God," Dashwood said. "You really want to know
the idea behind it all."

"Yes," DeAct said. "Certainly. That's our problem in a
nutshell."

"I don't go along with any of this, DeAct," Knight said.
"It's just a case of degeneracy and perversion, and who
cares what rationalizations they have?"

"That'll be enough, Tobias," DeAct repeated.

"I always say," Knight went on, " 'Scratch a scientist and
you'll find an atheist, and scratch an atheist and you'll find
a goddamned Commie."

"That will be *enough,* I said."

Dashwood was thinking. This was the old Mutt-and-Jeff
routine: the tough, dumb cop who terrified you, and the
smart, sympathetic cop who encouraged you to explain
yourself. Still . . .

"Very well," he said. "I will attempt to explain Project
Pan."

"You can call your lawyer before talking to us," DeAct
said hurriedly. "You can call a psychiatrist, too, if you
want," he added.

"I *am* a psychiatrist," Dashwood reminded him. Was
DeAct worried about the Supreme Court and the international repercussions of putting sixty-eight top scientists on
trial, or did he have some intuitive sense of the magnitude
of what Project Pan was all about?

"Can you take me seriously," Dashwood spoke directly
to DeAct, "if I tell you that what we have discovered here
is the summum bonum, the secret of secrets, the key to the
mystic powers of the ancients, the medicine of metals, the
stone of the wise, the lost art of the Rosicrucians . . . that
what you have been trained to consider most despicable is
the central sacrament of existence, the key to higher consciousness and intelligence, the evolutionary imperative, the
greatest scientific breakthrough of our epoch? Of course, I
always knew I would go to jail for it. I regard myself as
lucky to live in an age when you won't burn me at the
stake."

DeAct lit another cigarette, avoiding Dashwood's eyes.
He mumbled, "You sound a bit grandiose, Doctor."

"This guy's a schizo," Knight said, more bluntly.

"Let me begin at the beginning," Dashwood said, ignoring Knight. "We are all *primates*. Do you understand that, gentlemen?"

"Sure," DeAct said. "Evolution. I had that in college."

"It's just a theory," Knight grumbled. "A man still has the right to believe in God in this country, you know."

Knight was rather overdoing the tough-cop routine, Dashwood thought.

"It's a biochemical fact," Dashwood said, "that ninety-eight percent of our DNA is identical with chimpanzee DNA. Eighty-five percent of our DNA is identical with that of the South American spider monkey, our most distant relative in the primate family. That means, gentlemen, that most of our behavior is genetically programmed to follow the same survival, status, and sex programs as the other primates. We are only two percent different from the chimpanzee, and only fifteen percent different from the spider monkey. Think of that the next time you go to the zoo. Our cousins are looking out at us through the bars.

"Now let me emphasize this, gentlemen. We suffer from certain induced cultural hallucinations. Every tribe brainwashes its children into the island-reality of the adults of the tribe; that's the great discovery of Einstein in his principle of neurological relativism.

"In our tribe—Western Christian civilization, as it's called—we have brainwashed ourselves into not seeing and not thinking about our relationship to the other primates and to life in general. We know we are primates if we have gotten as far as college," he emphasized the last for Knight, "but we keep forgetting it, ignoring it, losing track of it."

"Bull*burger*," Knight growled. It was a typical primate reaction in a threat situation, Dashwood thought.

"Go on," DeAct said nervously, lighting a third cigarette.

"If I were to write a novel of about a thousand pages," Dashwood said, "and mentioned on every one of the first five hundred pages that all of us are primates, we would find it funny or satirical. Even stranger, if I stopped mentioning it for about two hundred pages, the readers would all forget it quickly, and be startled if I mentioned it again on page seven hundred. It's a fact that all educated persons *know,* but most of us would rather forget or simply not think about.

"Now, what is Bestiality, gentlemen?" Dashwood didn't pause, but answered his own question. "Sexual relations between a human and an animal. But humans are animals, as we keep forgetting, so that definition is culturally biased and self-serving. Bestiality is sex between animals, that's all. Inter-species sex. And any biologist will tell you that is quite common. Insects will Potter Stewart any bug that comes along if they can't find their own species. The ubiquity of the mule, gentlemen, shows how common is the occurrence of inter-species sex, Bestiality as our law calls it, between horses and donkeys. Throughout the reptile, bird, and fish kingdoms, the same behavior is commonplace.

"There is no species on the planet, gentlemen, that thinks it is 'degrading' to have sex with another species—except ourselves. And that is because we are trying to forget that we are primates."

Dashwood paused.

"This is some kind of put-on," Tobias Knight said irritably. "Get to the point, Dashwood."

But DeAct was crushing out his cigarette with a thoughtful frown. "So that's your defense, then?" he asked. "Scientific inquiry and so on. . . . You just wanted to find out the ah subjective similarities and differences in comparing Bestiality with ordinary sex and homosexuality and ah the other variations?"

"Defense!" Dashwood exclaimed. "I am not defending myself. Whether defense is necessary at all remains to be seen. Right now, I am merely filling you in on the background as you requested." He paused.

"All progress is made by violating taboos," he went on presently. "A certain friend of mine ah made that observation many years ago."

"Blake Williams," Tobias Knight said. "We know he's in this up to his ears."

"A *certain* friend," Dashwood went on, neither confirming nor denying. "He pointed out that without heretics and blasphemers—without rebels, that is—we would all still be living like Homo Erectus half a million years ago. All progress has been made by individuals who dared to think about the unthinkable and do the forbidden. As Oscar Wilde said: 'Disobedience was man's Original Virtue.' Those who dare—"

"Wilde was a Bryanting degenerate," Knight growled.

He was showing more of his canine teeth now: the signal of primate anger.

"Those who dare cross the line—any line—are explorers, and explorers sometimes get lost," Dashwood went on. "But without them, we never would have walked out of the tribal stage into the urban or out of the Dark Ages into the Renaissance.

"But enough rhetoric. Let me come to the point.

"Gentlemen, dozens of anthropologists have sat in this office and told me stories that once made my hair stand on end. And dozens, and scores, of parapsychologists have told me even wilder tales. Gentlemen, everybody outside Bad Ass or Seattle knows that the line between Experimental Music and Noise is very hard to find, that the line between avant-garde literature and nonsense is ambiguous, that even the line between the Beautiful and the Hideous is far from fixed, since a Ubangi woman with a plate in her lip is attractive to a Ubangi man, but absurd or repulsive to most of us. Mathematicians know that what constitutes proof is still not itself totally understood. Scientific Truth, so called, used to remain the same for millennia; then it began changing every century; in this century, it has changed every generation, and now seems to be changing every decade, or even quicker in some fields. And yet, in spite of all this, we think there is a firm, fixed, immutable boundary between the Real and the Unreal.

"Gentlemen, there is no such boundary.

"Everything that we regard as filthy, obscene, blasphemous, and disgusting is part of the ancient mind science called Magick."

Dashwood smiled gently. "Sex with a menstruating woman is forbidden, and considered 'indecent' or appalling, because it was once part of the sacraments of the Moon Goddess cult. The menstruating woman was thought to be possessed by the Goddess, I suppose, but the theory doesn't matter. Judeo-Christian civilization put the practice under a ban, and made it 'evil,' because it was part of the ancient Goddess religion that the worshippers of a Male God could not tolerate.

"Homosexuality is forbidden and considered revolting and ugly because it was part of the tradition of shamanism in most parts of the world not included in the Judeo-Christian cult.

177

"And yet, what do we find within the Judeo-Christian world itself? What do we find in the most orthodox times? We find secret cults using these forbidden acts for occult purposes. Sex with a menstruating woman was called 'the mystery of the Red Gold' by the alchemists, and was part of the process of consciousness expansion in that form of Magick. Homosexuality was part of the secret teachings of the Knights Templar and many other Magick cults."

"There are perverts everywhere," Knight said. "That doesn't prove anything."

Dashwood smiled again. "Tell me," he asked, "how do you feel after a good Potter Stewart?"

"What does that prove?" Knight demanded.

"Let us see where it leads us," Dashwood said. "You feel good, do you not? Yes, you will agree to that much. How would you feel after Potter Stewarting for four hours?"

"Tired."

"Not if you were trained in Tantra," Dashwood said. "Tantrists have been known to continue the sexual act for far longer—eight hours, even. Is it not strange that Shakespeare referred to it as 'the momentary trick,' and Kinsey found, back in the '40s, that the average Unistat male reaches Millett in less than two minutes? Is this not part of the Taboo I am discussing, the Taboo on the Magick secrets of non-Judeo-Christian religions? We have loosened up a lot since Kinsey's day, but to a Tantrist we are still rushing and missing the little details, you might say. Why is that?"

DeAct lit still another cigarette. "Jesus," he said, "are you telling us that every kind of sex that's forbidden in the Bible is the key to some kind of occult knowledge or power? Is that it?"

"A long time ago, when I wasn't ready to understand yet," Dashwood said, "a parapsychologist told me, 'Scratch a trance medium and you'll find a homosexual.' That's not one hundred percent true, but it's true more often than not.

"The Moon Goddess is a metaphor, let us say. But what happens to a woman in her menses, the power that is present and can be used in mind science, is no metaphor.

"Now, what started Project Pan was that I discovered, by 'accident' as they say, just browsing in a book that didn't seem to relate to my own work at all, a book on Egypt, and there it was: there was a priestess who performed fellatio on a goat every year on the Egyptian New Year's

Day, which is our July 23. Yes, gentlemen—in the vernacular, she gave the goat a Steinem-Job."

"There are perverts everywhere," Knight repeated.

"This was central to the Egyptian religion," Dashwood said. "Was the whole religion a perversion? Don't you see, everything called perversion got that name because it was part of the old Magick tradition?

"And guess what, gentlemen: What is the most common subject in the cave paintings left by our ancestors thirty thousand years ago?

"Bestiality. Yes, gentlemen—our ancestors portrayed themselves, over and over, having sex with goats and bisons and every animal they knew about."

"I don't believe it," Knight said flatly.

"Look it up sometime," Dashwood said pleasantly. "It's mentioned in *Ghost Dance: Origins of Religion,* by Weston LeBarre, one of our most respected anthropologists. You never see those paintings in any popular books of cave art, but every paleo-anthropologist knows about them.

"You find the same in ancient Indian art, ancient Babylonian art, ancient art everywhere.

"And you find the Magick secret coded into myth and legend over and over. The formula for producing a Man-God or Super-Hero is the mating of human and animal. Europa and the bull; Leda and the swan; Beauty and the Beast; the Buddha fathered by a white elephant in some versions of the legend.

"Tantric sex is the portal of the mysteries, and the alchemists called it the secret of silver. *This* is the secret of gold, gentlemen. And it's even coded into the Judeo-Christian mythos—after the Gnostics got through editing the manuscripts. Why do you think Eve and the Serpent are credited with giving us the knowledge of good and evil? Why does the Hebrew word for 'serpent,' *neschek,* have the same Cabalistic value as the word 'Messiah'? Why is the Messiah born of the union of a *woman with a bird?* Can't you read the message in the formula, *animal-human-super-human?*"

"This is blasphemous and disgusting, as well as criminal," Knight said. "You, Dr. Dashwood, are as crazy as a loon."

"Why do you feel 'good' during and after sex?" Dashwood went on. "Just nature's way of tricking us into reproducing the species? Yes, that is part of it. But nature loves to economize, to do several things at once. You feel high and powerful because you are raising your mental energy—the *Kundalini* of the Hindu metaphor. With the proper ritual and proper training, the energy can be raised to the point where your Will and Imagination are illuminated with power and you can create a new Reality. Literally. You walk over the line between the state marked 'real' as far as you dare to go into the 'unreal,' and you make a new line. Until you have the courage to try again and go even farther out . . ."

"Crazy as a loon," Knight repeated.

DeAct put out his cigarette and lit another. "I want to thank you, Dr. Dashwood," he said formally, "for being so open with us and ah taking us into your confidence so fully. You will understand, of couse, that we cannot ah buy your argument at ah first glance. It is startling and ah very unorthodox and ah that is, well, I'm sure the jury will understand, a brilliant mind and probably the factor of overwork and too much imagination."

Dashwood stood up. "I see," he said. "Well, it's time I tried it—the one experiment I was always afraid of."

"Grab him, Tobias!" DeAct shouted.

But he was too late.

Dashwood opened his mouth to its maximum extension, breathed in deeply, and then bellowed:

IIOZA

KHOEO

OOYTH

OEAZA

EAOOZ

AKHOZ

AKHEY

THXAA

LETHY

KH

"Gesundheit," Knight said automatically.
But Dashwood was gone from that universe.

The sign said:

CHAPEL PERILOUS
PRICE OF ADMISSION: YOUR MIND
S. MUSS SINE, PROPRIETOR

Dashwood passed through the lavatory into the laboratory, where Patrick Knowles and Lon Chaney were turning switches and throwing relays wildly as Bela Lugosi, with Karloff's old makeup, tried to pretend he was the Frankenstein monster, while Ilona Masey huddled in a corner, looking worried.

"You want next door," General Crowley told him.

But next door was a stark white-and-black room, with a photograph—or a view—of the central galaxy, and a large penny-farthing bicycle standing under the eye-in-the-pyramid.

"Where am I?" Dashwood asked.

"In the village."

"What do you want?"

"Negative entropy."

"Which side are you on?" he demanded.

"That would be telling."

It seemed that some refurbishing and rebuilding had been going on in the downtown area, for Union Square was much bigger than Dashwood remembered and there were several new buildings surrounding it, most of them built in hyperbolic and non-Euclidean curves. Chinatown was now facing directly onto the Square instead of being two blocks downhill and to the right, but there was a huge sign on the Chinatown Gate, saying:

CLOSED FOR ALTERATIONS
FU MANCHU, PROPRIETOR

Claude Shannon of Bell Laboratories and Tristan Tzara, the pioneer Dadaist, were picking random words out of people's mouths as they passed and gluing them to a huge billboard where they had already formed the pseudosentence:

AMERICAN LIFE BOMB WENT AUTHORITARIAN
IN FRONTAL ATTACK ON AN ENGLISH AUTHOR.

"We're discovering the information/redundance ratio in random signals," Shannon explained, waving a programmable calculator.

"We're creating a new Art Form!" Tzara shouted.

"This is the lower astral," Cary Grant said, materializing from the feet up until he was all there, but in black-and-white. "In fact, most of the characters around here are only half-astral."

The Tin Woodsman of Oz went by, with some of the boys from the Heavy Metal Mob.

"How long does this go on?" Disk asked. The voices were pounding in his head: YOU ARE GEORGE DORN YOU ARE GEORGE DORN YOU ARE GEORGE DORN

There were only two doors leading back out to the Bureau of Common Sense. One had a picture of Christ on the cross and bore the legend, LOVE ONE ANOTHER; but the other had a picture of Captain Ahab and bore the legend, I'D STRIKE THE SUN IF IT INSULTED ME.

"Do I have to make a choice?" Babbitt asked. All this was going by too fast for him—one minute he was driving home from work and passed the billboard on Howard Street with the eye-in-the-pyramid, and the next minute he was in this place.

"I'll never smoke this stuff again," George Dorn decided.

The lights began to go out all over San Francisco, first in ones and twos, then in dozens and scores, and then in hundreds, until a stygian blackness descended in which Punk Rock groups and transvestites could be seen dimly as they marched in robot hordes toward the Bay.

"UFO's over the power stations!" somebody shouted. "A major blackout!"

"It's only a Natural Phenomenon," somebody else urged, trying to quiet the spreading panic.

But out of the night and the fog a huge pair of Brownmillers gradually became apparent, hanging over the City like two Goodyear Blimps in a nosedive.

And behind the locked gate of Chinatown the drums of Fu Manchu began.

The Punk Rock groups led the parade downhill, through Chinatown, to the Ocean.

"Turn back, turn back!" screamed an effete intellectual snob. "The sea is NOT our home! Beware of the rising rivers of blood, beware of the Robot Animal Within. Turn back, turn back!"

But the Punkers marched, and everybody fell in step behind them. First came the Ludes and the Creepers, then the Dirks and the Blunt Instruments, then more and more: the Problem of Anxiety, the Daggers, the Funny Farm, the Noon's Repose, and the Troubled Midnight. And now it was not separate trickles, but one huge rushing stream: the Leapers, the Laughing Academy, the Foamix Culprits, the Mail Cover, Dr. Terror's House of Ill Repute, the Keyhole Peepers, the Wire Tappers, the Whoopee Casket Company. And over the shrieks and howls of their music, from deep inside the hidden recesses of Chinatown, the drums of Fu Manchu grew louder.

And more and more were coming, still: Dashwood recognized the Muggers, the Synthesizers, Moses and Monotheism, Reefer Madness, Crazy Artie's Crisis Intervention Center, the Junior College of Cardinals, Totem and Taboo, the Things on the Doorstep, the Hoods, the Lanovacs, Six Flags over the Vatican, the Sleepers, the Beepers, the Roofers, the Cokers, the Thundering Hoofs, the Framis Stand, the Power to Cloud Men's Minds, and the Croakers.

Pickering's Moon circled the Earth, going backward.

And still the Punks came: the Chocolate Mouse, the Tax Writeoff, the Welfare Bums, the Primal Scream, Baphomet's Witnesses, the Black Rabbit of Inlé, the Vegetables, the Fruits, the Nuts, the First Church of Satan Scientist, the Tantric Presbyterians, the Huns, the Creatures from the Back Ward, the Special Children, the Visigoths, the Vandals, the Looters, the Shooters, the Scooters, the Peanut Butter Conspiracy Revisited, the Thousand Kim, the Seeds of Discord, the Benton Harbor Rat-Weasel, the Bloodshot Pyramid, the Wascal Wabbits, Crescendo, the Diabolic Variations, Skinnerball, the Committee for the Elimination of Death, the Weird Made Flesh, the Poor Golems, the Wretched Refuse, the Alluminum Bavariati, the Double Helix, the Goons, the Thugs, the Teeming Shore, the Unnatural Act, the Solitary Vice, the Morose Delectation, the Wrist Slashers, the Window Jumpers, the Kryptonite

Kids, the Stay-Free Mini-Pads, the Elect Cohens, the Corpse-Eaters of Leng, the Miniature Sled, the Hash Brownies, the Boston Blackies, Kadath in the Cold Waste, the Neanderthal Tails, the Giant Slugs, the Sloths, the Disadvantaged Youth, the Albert de Salvo Fan Club, the Dead Kennedys, the Molotov Cocktails, and, loudest and most eldritch of all, Great Cthulhu's Starry Wisdom Band.

And overall there was a smell of fried onions.

Ying Kaw Foy leaned above him, blouse open, those breasts like ripe apricots dangling like the forbidden fruit on the Tree of Knowledge.

"Kiss them," she begged. "Kiss them; don't leave me, you foolish old man. . . ."

He managed to raise himself, to mouth one nipple, and then he went, he went, he went, into the n-dimensional Klein bottle again.

Hierusalem, my happy home,
When shall I come to thee?
When shall my sorrows have an end,
Thy joys when shall I see?

Thy walls are made of precious stones
Thy bulwarks diamonds square
Thy gates are of right orient pearl
Exceeding rich and rare

There trees for evermore bear fruit
And evermore do spring;
There evermore the angels sit
And evermore do sing

Ah, my sweet home, Hierusalem,
Would God I were in thee!
Would God my woes were at an end
Thy joys that I might see

It was dark in the room. His mother sang that song. She wore a perfume that smelled like lily-of-the-valley.

Dashwood cut through an alley where two ancient Egyptian priestesses were leading a captured UFOnaut in chains past a Dog-Headed God.

"Maybe Acid would help," somebody muttered.

SDATE YOUR BIZNIZ PLEEZ, the computer insisted. HOOKUP UZING IMPROVED EQUIPMEND TO AVOID FEEDBACK. SDAY TUNED.

A North Beach barker was haranguing the crowd from a platform. Dashwood noticed that he wore a ribbon declaring him the GOLD WINNER of 1984 Bad Ass Texas Hog Calling Contest. YOU'VE GOT TO HAVE APPEAL AS WELL AS POWER IN YOUR VOICE, he was thundering. YOU HAVE TO CONVINCE THE SWINE THAT YOU HAVE WHAT THEY NEED. YES, FOLKS, THIS IS A TOTALLY UNIQUE EXPERIENCE IN LIVING ALTERNATVES—EDUCATIONAL, PERSONAL, RECREATIONAL, SOCIAL, AND HEDONIC. YOU CAN EXPLORE MEXICO, THE PACIFIC OCEAN, AND YOUR OWN SEXUAL POTENTIAL ON THIS CRUISE, VISIT LEMURIA, ATLANTIS, AND THE BISEXUAL APES OF MU—

He was hit by a passing truck labeled BLESSINGS DIAPER SERVICE, and as he struggled to get to his feet, another truck labeled ABC BABY SERVICE ran over him again. The crowd groaned.

A Dominican monk marched past carrying a sign that said:

JEWES WE KILLE
TO SERVE GOD'S WILLE

Strange messages were appearing on the computer console: SL LR MS ASK GREEN DREAMS TK X1826PCS M.Y.O.B. (MIND YOUR OWN BUSINESS)

Simon Moon seized the microphone and began a long, unintelligible speech about the Drug Problem. In each of our major cities, he seemed to be saying, there are thousands of people who desperately need dope. For all practical purposes these people simply cannot live unless they get "high." He estimated the number of afflicted adults in the nation at well over 125,000,000, and said their habits included, but were not limited to, Valium, marijuana, Miltown, uppers, downers, acid, cigarettes, booze, aspirin, DMT, cocaine, peyote, and Coca-Cola. He called upon all concerned citizens to donate their surplus dope to a huge pile in the center of each city, to be called the Public Trough, from which the needy could take what was necessary to keep them functioning.

The window next door lit up suddenly, showing an ancient Hindu princess in Tantric rapture with a UFOnaut.

"Eternal Serpent Power," Simon was ranting. "If we all raise the *Kundalini* at once, maybe we can get through the Dark Night of the Soul and see the Golden Dawn. Three A.M. is the worst of it—that's the peak for UFO Contacts, murders, suicides, and Bad Trips."

A brutal group of Cro-Magnons came over the hill and began clubbing Ancient Astronauts to death. The Cro-Magnons were tall, blonde, and Aryan; the Astronauts had the blue skin of Krishna and Quetzalcoatl.

A neon sign flashed:

HALL OF SELF-LOVE
THE AMERICAN DREAM ACHIEVED
DO WHAT THOU WILT SHALL BE THE WHOLE OF THE LAW

In the first room, George Washington was holding a movie camera on Linda Lovelace as she masturbated and moaned, staring fixedly into the camera-eye. In the second room, John Adams was holding a movie camera on Georgina Spelvin as she masturbated and moaned, staring fixedly into the camera-eye. In the third room, Thomas Jefferson was holding a movie camera on Annette Haven as she masturbated and moaned, staring fixedly into the camera-eye. In the fourth room, James Madison was holding a movie camera on Tina Russell as she masturbated and moaned, staring fixedly into the camera-eye.

"What's the use of revolution without general masturbation?" sang a Punk Rock group called Dr. Climax's House of Dildos.

In the fifth room James Monroe was holding a movie

camera on Marilyn Chambers as she masturbated and moaned, staring fixedly into the camera-eye, so it would register every expression in her eyes, every involuntary twitch of pleasure around her mouth.

A spastic handed Dashwood a leaflet headed "HELP EPILEPTICS LIVE AND WORK IN DIGNITY."

A girder fell on the one just man in San Francisco.

Anarchists ran through the streets screaming, *"Aux armes, citoyens!* The government is taking over our country!"*

CLEAR FOR LAW AND ORDER DAY GREETING! blared the loudspeakers. FOLLOWING IS GREETING FOR LAW-AND-ORDER DAY.

Cotton Mather, Cotton Hawes, and Cotten DeAct paraded past with a sign saying:

YE POPE TO SHUNNE
A BATTLE WUNNE

A girder fell on an unjust man.

George Dorn realized that, amid all this nightmare imagery from the random circuits, he was coming back together again, a little bit at a time, coming out of the illusion that he was Frank Dashwood.

"Here it is," Cagliostro the Great said, handing George a book called *The Answer.*

George opened the volume eagerly. It had one page and said:

FLOSSING

"Here it is," Dr. Hugh Crane said, handing George a book called *The Answer*.

Frank opened the volume eagerly. It had one page and said:

> Jan Zelenka was born in Bohemia in 1679, wrote in a style similar to [and much admired by] Johann Sebastian Bach, died in 1745. Much of his sacred music is still admired, but perhaps his greatest composition was his *Capriccio* of 1723.

"Here it is," Eva Gebloomenkraft said, handing him a book called *The Answer*.

It blew up in his hand like a loaded cigar.

She appeared to Marvin Gardens reclining upon a golden bed, and Her hair was spendidly red and She was naked and wanton and unashamed; on Her face was the narrow-eyed bliss of Kali, and one hand was opening the lips of Her Feinstein as She pleasured Herself. She was on page sixty-four of *Penthouse*.

To Hassan i Sabbah X, She was literally the Black Mother, Mistress of creation and destruction, and he adored Her in his own fashion.

Epicene Wildeblood willed with all his heart and all his mind to become one with Her, to be Her; and the surgeons obliged him.

To Dodgson, She was ever the Child, forever innocent, beyond logic and beyond every paradox; and She led him to the doors of Wonderland.

For all of Her lovers go mad, by the standards of the world; but it is not so; it is the world that is mad, and melancholy, and murderous, because it does not know Her and love Her.

And summer's lease hath all too short a date.

"It's not God; it's not Goddess; it's not even the Mad Fishmonger or the Invisible Hand," he decided after the fifth toke. "By Golly, it *is* the Tooth Fairy!"

Out of the sea rose a gigantic, chryselephantine, bodacious, incredible yellow submarine, waving the Black Flag of Anarchy and the Golden Apple of Discord.

Mavis, the woman with the tommy gun, appeared at a window. "Gravity sucks!" she shouted. "The cream of the jest rises to the top. That's the Law of Levity."

And the submarine took off and floated over North Beach like a flying saucer.

Mavis threw down a rope. "Grab hold, George!" she shouted. "We've come to rescue you!"

And he leaped, and grabbed hold, and they pulled him up, into the Golden Space Ship.

Captain Hagbard Celine (who looked a lot like Hugh Crane the magician, when you stopped to think about it, and a little bit like Harry Coin, the crazy assassin, and somewhat like Everyman) took his hand. "Good to have you back aboard, George. Was it rough down there?"

He tried to be modest. "Well, you know how it is on primitive planets. . . ."

"They gave you merry hell," Hagbard said. "I can see it in your face. Well, cheer up, George. It's over now. We're heading home."

And indeed there were thousands, maybe hundreds of thousands, of them: great golden ships sailing past the speed of light, heading into the center of the galaxy.

It was the planetary birth process; earth, like a single giant flower, after incubating for four billion years, was discharging its seed.

And the ships, like homing pigeons, were going back where the experiment began, where the DNA was created and ejaculated out onto every planet, where the Star Makers dwell, beyond the Black Hole, out of space, out of time.

And he woke up.

He looked at the alarm clock blearily, still haunted by spaceships and quantum jumps. Six-fifty-eight: the alarm would go off in two mintues.

He was aware of the readers, waiting for him to remember who he really was and what universe he was really in.

He was aware of the Novelist, too, also waiting to see what he would do and what he would think.

He crawled out of bed and raised the window shade, letting the dawn sun in.

He sat at the typewriter.

He pecked out, slowly, thinking of it, one letter at a time:

YOU ALL GET ONE VOTE
THE UNIVERSE IS CREATED BY THE PAR-
TICIPATION OF THE PARTICIPANTS
TODAY IS THE FIRST DAY OF THE REST OF
THE UNIVERSE

He thought a little more and added, as one last act of defiance against all T.H.E.M.:

I AM NOT GEORGE DORN. I WILL DECIDE
WHO AND WHAT I AM.

It still wouldn't do.
He wrote a final chapter.

THE RETURN TO ITHACA

The future exists first in Imagination, then in Will, then in Reality.

—Barbara Marx Hubbard

One evening while Wing Chee was meditating, he found himself floating higher and higher, becoming more and more detached, observing with total lucidity that he was a little old man sitting in a room high on a hill over a huge city on a planet circling around a star in a galaxy of myriads of stars among countless galaxies extending to infinity and eternity in all directions, within his own mind.

And in that lucidity he knew that he had been lying to himself for months, pretending not to notice what was happening to his body as it gradually terminated its basic functions, fearful of looking straight at Death; but now, in that lucidity, looking at it and seeing that it was just another of the millions of things that Wing Chee (who was so rich and powerful) could not do anything about; but now, in that lucidity and objectivity, looking far down at this particular galaxy, this insignificant solar system, this temporary city, this house that a strong wind could blow away, this absurd old man who was rich and powerful but could not command the tides or alter the paths of the stars, it was all suddenly a great joke and every little detail made sense. For, in this new lucidity and objectivity and selfless perspective, he did not giggle or weep or feel dazed, but only smiled, very slightly, knowing he would soon lose this body, which was like an old rundown car, and this central nervous system, which was like a tired and increasingly incompetent driver, and the metaprogrammer in the higher nervous centers which gave him this perspective, because out here be-

yond space-time he simply did not give a damn about that
life, that planet, or that universe anymore.

So, as he very slowly came down, contracted, into Euclidean 3D again, he was aware of every amusing, poignant, radiant little detail, the wholeness and the harmony
and the luminosity of it all, knowing how richly he would
enjoy every last minute of it, now that it didn't matter to
him anymore.

The next day, he called the office and told his secretary
he wouldn't be in. Then he took a long walk, enjoying
every bird, every flower, every blade of grass, every radiant
detail, and getting a bit winded—another sign that the car
was running down—and finally taking a cab to Ying Kaw
Foy's house.

She wept when he told her, but he smiled and joked and
chided her out of it.

"I may be one of the last men to die," he said, when she
was calm. "President Hubbard in Unistat is putting a lot of
money into research on longevity and immortality. No,
don't weep again; it is nothing to me. I feel like one of the
last dinosaurs."

"You are the best man in the world," she said, eyes flashing.

"I have been good to *you*," he said. "I have been as much
of a scoundrel as was necessary to be rich and comfortable.
Many will be glad of my death."

He told of how he was arranging to have most of his
estate liquidated, turned into cash, and deposited in her account.

He urged her to take advantage of the longevity drugs as
they became available, and to meditate every day. "One
year of life is wonderful, when you are conscious of the details. A thousand years would be more wonderful." And
then he added a strange thing: "Think of me sometimes,
and look for me. You'll never see old Wing Chee again, but
you'll see what I *really* am if you look hard enough and
long enough."

And then suddenly he realized it was coming even
sooner than he had expected. "How absurd," he said. "I
must lie down now."

He stretched out on her couch. "I must have walked too
far," he said. "So many hills . . . so many ups and downs
. . . and all I want now is one thing. Open your blouse,

193

please. That's right, thank you. No, I just want to look at them. Such lovely Brownmillers, like peaches. Let me touch them. No, let me kiss them. No, never mind, I'm going now."

"Don't go," she cried. "Kiss them, kiss them first."

"Right back where I started," he said, suckling. And then he left her.

Ms. Ying decided to go to the French Riviera, after the funeral. She would spend a year there, having a series of young, crude, unintelligent lovers (who wouldn't remind her of him) and then decide what to do with her money and the rest of her life.

She sold the Rehnquist and a lot of other junk when she gave up her house in Hong Kong.

The wholesaler didn't know what to do with the Rehnquist at first, but he finally sold it to a Sex Shop in Yokohama.

Markoff Chaney, a Machiavellian midget, was vacationing in Japan that summer, because—after years of paying him only about three hundred dollars a month—his stocks in Blue Sky, Inc., were suddenly paying two thousand dollars or three thousand dollars a month.

Blue Sky made zero-gravity devices that were proving very useful in the space cities President Hubbard had created.

Chaney had also written a book, which was selling moderately well despite its rather eccentric thesis. It was his endeavor to prove that all the great achievements in art, science, and culture were the work of persons who were, on the average, less than five feet tall, and often shorter. He claimed that this fact had been "covered up" by what he called "unconscious sizist prejudice" on the part of professional historians.

He had called the book *Little Men with Big Balls*, but the publisher, out of a sense that Chaney perhaps had some unconscious prejudice of his own and certainly lacked good taste, had changed the title to *Little People with Big Ideas*.

Chaney spent his first day in Japan visiting Kyoto. He went out to see where the Temple of the Golden Pavilion had once stood, and he spent three hours walking around there, trying to get into the head of the Zen monk who had burned it down.

Chaney had known the story for years: how the monk, working on the *koan*, "Does a dog have the Buddha Nature?," had tried one answer after another, always getting hit upside the head by his *Roshi* and told he didn't have it yet. Finally, after meditating continuously for a day and a half without sleep or food, the monk had a brainstorm of some kind and dashed from his cell with a hell of a yell and burned down the Temple, the most beautiful building in Japan at the time.

The court had declared the monk insane.

After three hours of trying to get into the monk's headspace when he set fire to the building, Chaney had his own brainstorm. He had been ignoring Dr. Dashwood for three or four months, he realized.

He took a cab to Western Union and dispatched a telegram to Dr. Dashwood at Orgasm Research. It said:

> **FLOSSING IS THE ANSWER**
> **EZRA POUND**

Chaney had gotten those words many months ago, while having some dental work done. The dentist had suggested they try nitrous oxide, and Chaney eagerly agreed.

He remembered that the great psychologist, William James, had once thought he had the whole secret of the

Universe on a nitrous oxide trip. What James had written down, in trying to verbalize his insight, was: OVERALL THERE IS A SMELL OF FRIED ONIONS. Chaney wanted to know what it was like to be in the state where fried onions would explain everything. He sniffed deeply and expectantly as the mask was placed over his nose, and waited.

No illumination came at first, but the room seemed to be getting bigger and bigger, and then it was getting smaller and smaller, and then he became aware that the dentist, as was typical of his species, was making remonstrating noises as he gazed into Chaney's mouth, saying that brushing was not enough and that everybody should be more conscious of dental hygiene and so on, all the usual craperoo, and then he, Chaney, wasn't there anymore, he wasn't anywhere; it was just like what he had heard about quantum jumping in physics, because he was there again, having gone from 0 to 1, and then going back to 0 again, not being there, and then back to 1 again and the dentist said somberly, like a very wise old wizard:

"Flossing is the answer."

And Chaney felt like he might giggle or weep, but was too dazed to do either, having found it at last, the Answer. And it was so simple, as all the mystics said; it was right out in the open and we didn't notice it because we weren't conscious of the details. And he stared up, awed, at the wise face of the great sage who had given it to him, at last, the Answer.

Flossing.

And the damnedest part of it was that for weeks after he still had flashes when he thought that was it, the Answer. Flossing.

After Kyotó, Chaney went to Yokohama to see the infamous Sex Shops, as was inevitable.

He had a Sex Problem almost as big as his ego. He lusted after the Giant Women (the statistical, that is to say, the fictitious majority), but he was also afraid of them, because they might think he was ridiculous.

A large part of his book, in fact, was devoted to veiled (and sometimes not so veiled) hints that shorter-than-average men had larger-than-average equipment and were actually extraordinarily passionate lovers. He claimed, of course, that this had been ignored or covered up, due to "unconscious sizist prejudice."

In the first Sex Shop he purchased an artificial vagina which seemed vastly superior, in both realism and pneumatic grip, to the model he had at home.

In the second Sex Shop he bought a box of pornographic Easter Eggs.

By then he was feeling the surging despair again, knowing that these substitutes were not what he really wanted, knowing his loneliness and his exile with that bitterness that he usually kept at bay by concentrating on the absurdity of everything-in-general, experiencing the terrible isolation of being out there on the moon separated from the ridiculous oversized clods by 250,000 miles of sizist prejudice.

And then, in the third Sex Shop, he found it.

The Answer.

And it wasn't flossing at all.

Dr. Glopberger had worked in the Sex Change department of Johns Hopkins for a long time, and thought that nothing could surprise him any longer.

Markoff Chaney surprised him.

"No," Chaney said, in answer to the first question Glopberger always asked, "I've never felt like a woman trapped in a man's body."

"Um," Glopberger said. "Well, sir, what *do* you want here?"

Chaney opened the box in his lap.

"Good God," Glopberger said. "I've only seen one *that* big once in my life." What was that character's name—Wildebeeste? Strange one: he had kept it after the operation, had it mounted on a plaque or something like that.

"You see," Chaney explained, "I don't want to become a woman. I want to become more of a man."

"Well," said Dr. Glopberger, professionally. "Well, well." It was an ingenious challenge, even with the advances in Sex Surgery in the past three years, but it could be done. . . . My word, it would be a Medical First.

The stocks in Blue Sky were now paying eight thousand dollars to ten thousand dollars a month.

"Name your price," Chaney said with a steely glint.

Justin Case heard about the man with no name at one of Mary Margaret Wildeblood's wild, wild parties. Joe Malik, the editor of *Confrontation,* told the story. It was rather hard for Case to follow because the party was huge and noisy—a typical Wildeblood *soirée.* All the usual celebrities were there—Blake Williams, the most boring crank in the galaxy; Juan Tootrego, the rocket engineer responsible for the first three space cities; Carol Christmas, the man who had invented the first longevity drug, *Ex-Tend;* Natalie Drest, the fiery feminist; Bertha Van Ation, the astronomer who had discovered the first real Black Hole, in the Sirius double-star system; Markoff Chaney, the midget millionaire who owned most of Blue Sky, Inc. Hordes of other Names —maxi-, midi-, and mini-celebrities—swarmed through Mary Margaret's posh Sutton Place pad as the evening wore on. There was a lot of booze, a lot of hash, and—due to Chaney—altogether too much coke.

"The town was called Personville," Malik was saying, "and the man with no name was a detective for a big agency like Pinkerton's. But then Kurasawa adapted it, and the man with no name became a Samurai."

"Of course we can go to the stars," Markoff Chaney was saying, even louder, on Case's other side. "The speed of light doesn't mean a thing when you consider what the next two or three jumps in longevity will bring. There are no real limits anywhere, except in the thinking of the timid and the conservative." He was armed with new Courage.

"Then he became Clint Eastwood," Malik said.

"What's your game?" Juan Tootrego asked, making conversation.

"Oh, art," Case said. "I write the art column in *Confrontation*."

"But he still didn't have a name!" Malik exclaimed.

"Then you're the man who discovered El Mir," Juan Tootrego said, impressed. Blake Williams snickered suddenly.

"Everybody this is Simon Moon the President's husband," Mary Margaret said.

The First Man fidgeted in their gaze.

"I'm not here to do any electioneering," he said.

"He's one of the best chess players in the country," Mary Margaret said, completing the introduction.

"Um how does it feel to be married to a politician?" Case asked, trying to put Simon at ease.

"Eve has her thing, and I have mine," Simon said.

"I have a theory," Blake Williams orated, "that the chessboard is a model of the human brain. What do you think of that, Mtr. Hubbard?"

"Mt. Moon," Simon said quickly. He was a Masculinist.

"You see," Malik went on, "whether he's a detective, a Samurai, or a cowboy, he still has no name. Isn't that archetypal?"

"I always look at the bright side," Hagbard Celine was saying to Natalie Drest. "There's only 337,665 years to go in the Kali Yuga, for instance."

"Well, if Batman is so smart," Marvin Gardens muttered, "why does he wear his underdrawers outside of his pants?"

"Pardon me," Simon Moon was asking Blake Williams, "but did you say Grand Canyon should be considered as an artistic whole or as an artistic hole?"

"Why, yes," Markoff Chaney was telling Mary Margaret, "I *am* working on a second book. It's called *Reality Is What You Can Get Away With,* and it's about the future evolution of consciousness and intelligence." His Courage was growing.

"Child-proof bottles, my Abzug," Marvin Gardens complained. "There isn't a child in the world who doesn't have the patience and curiosity to open one of them."

"He has no name," Malik said, "because he is Death, and Death is a nightmare from which humanity is beginning to awaken."

"It's time to stop worshipping gods," Chaney went on earnestly, "and aim at becoming gods. It took four and a half billion years to produce this moment, and who's really awake yet?"

"It's adults who give up on the damned bottles," Marvin Gardens went on. "They decide—I know I do—'Agh, the hell, I don't *need* the Potter Stewarting pills.' What they are is *adult-proof* bottles."

"Who *is* that exciting man?" Natalie Drest whispered to Mary Margaret.

"Marvin Gardens, the brain surgeon. He's married to Dr. Lovelace the uh you know the first woman Bishop in the Mormon Church."

Benny Benedict; the columnist, arrived, apologizing for being late. "I had to see my mother at the Senior Citizens' home. Great old gal, she's taken up tennis again since she started on *Ex-Tend*."

"Well, yes," Hagbard Celine was saying. "I was a stage magician in my youth. Called myself Cagliostro the Great. But then I got turned on to Cabala. . . ."

"Everybody this is John Disk he's the assistant to Dr. Lousewart at NASA-Ames. . . ."

"No wife, no horse, no mustache," General Wing Chee (U.S. Army, ret.) was saying. "I really resented that."

And then everybody else had left and they were alone.

"Of course there are robots among us," Chaney said, finishing his last speech. "There are also Magicians among us. I think we take turns playing each role, as a matter of fact. The Magician defines a reality-mesh and the robot lives in it. Grok?"

"God, you're an attractive man," Mary Margaret breathed, thinking of his Courage.

Their eyes locked. Because of the magnetism of his personality, neither of them was conscious of the fact that she was looking a long way down at him.

"Let's sniff a little more coke," Chaney suggested.

"I have some cognac left, too," she whispered.

"Perfect," he said, and quoted:

> Heart of my heart, come out of the rain,
> Soak me in cognac, love and cocaine!

They went to the kitchen to get the cognac, and he was swaggering a bit, like Perry Mason about to cross-examine, or the new gun in town.

He patted her Frankel gently. She patted his new Courage.

Then they went to the bedroom, and—after circumnavigating the globe and passing through 10^{23} possible universes—Ulysses finally returned to Ithaca.

GLOSSARY:
A GUIDE FOR THE PERPLEXED

BELL'S THEOREM: A mathematical demonstration by Dr. John S. Bell, which shows that if quantum mechanics is valid, any two particles once in contact will continue to influence each other, no matter how far apart they may subsequently move. This violates Special Relativity, unless the "influence" between the particles is not employing any known energy. This is the "form" in Spencer Brown's sense of *The Trick Top Hat.*

COPENHAGEN INTERPRETATION: The theory formulated by Niels Bohr, according to which the *state vector* (see below) should be regarded as a mathematical formalism. In other words —which some physicists will dispute—the equations of quantum mechanics do not describe what is happening in the sub-atomic world but what mathematical systems *we need to create* to think of that world.

COSMIC GLUE: A metaphor to describe the quantum interconnectedness that must exist if Bell's Theorem be valid. Coined by Dr. Nick Herbert.

EIGENSTATE: One of a finite number of states that a quantum system can be in. The Superposition Principle says that, before measurement, a system must be considered to be in all of its eigenstates; measurement selects one eigenstate.

EINSTEIN-ROSEN-PODOLSKY EFFECT: The quantum interconnectedness as described in a paper by Einstein, Rosen, and Podolsky. The purpose of said paper was to prove that quantum mechanics cannot be valid, since it leads to such an outlandish conclusion. Since Bell's Theorem, some physicists have chosen to accept the interconnectedness, however outlandish it may seem. See QUIP.

EVERETT-WHEELER-GRAHAM MODEL: An alternative to Bell's Theorem and the Copenhagen Interpretation. According to Everett, Wheeler, and Graham, everything that can happen to the state vector (see below) does happen to it. This is the Brownian "form" of *The Universe Next Door*.

FORM: In the sense of G. Spencer Brown, a mathematical or logical system necessary to systematic thought but having the inevitable consequence of imposing its own deep structures upon the experiences packaged and indexed by the form. See CO-PENHAGEN INTERPRETATION.

HIDDEN VARIABLE: An alternative to Bell, Copenhagen, and Everett-Wheeler-Graham. As developed by Dr. David Bohm, the Hidden Variable theory assumes that quantum events are determined by a sub-quantum system acting outside or before the universe of space-time known to us. Dr. Evan Harris Walker and Dr. Nick Herbert have suggested that the Hidden Variable is consciousness; Dr. Jack Sarfatti suggests that it is *information*.

INFORMATION: A measure of the unpredictability of a message; that is, the more unpredictable a message is, the more information it contains. Since systems tend to disorder (according to the second law of thermodynamics), we can think of the degree of order in a system as the amount of information in it. Ordinarily information is transmitted as an ordering of energy (a signal), in which the energy and its ordering (the message) is transmitted from one place to another. Dr. Jack Sarfatti has suggested that the non-locality of the ERP effect and Bell's Theorem may entail the instantaneous transfer of order from one place to another *without any energy transfer*. Thus we can have both Bell's Theorem and Special Relativity, since Special Relativity only prohibits the instantaneous transfer of energy and does not say anything about instantaneous transfer of information.

NEURO-: A prefix denoting "known or mediated by the nervous system." Since all human knowledge is neurological in this sense, every science may be considered a neuro-science; e.g., we have no physics but neuro-physics, no psychology but neuro-psychology and, ultimately, no neurology but neuro-neurology. But neuro-neurology would itself be known by the nervous system, leading to neuro-neuro-neurology etc., in an infinite regress. See VON NEUMANN'S CATASTROPHE.

NON-LOCAL: Not dependent upon space and time. A non-local effect occurs instantaneously and with no attenuation due to distance. Special Relativity seems to forbid all such non-local effects, but Bell's Theorem seems to show that quantum mechanics demands them. The only solutions thus far offered to this contradiction are that non-local effects involve "consciousness" rather than energy (Walker, Herbert) or that they involve "information" rather than energy (Sarfatti).

NON-OBJECTIVITY: One of the two alternatives to Bell's Theorem (the other being the Everett-Wheeler-Graham model). In order to avoid non-locality, some physicists such as Dr. John A. Wheeler prefer this option, which holds that the universe has no reality aside from observation. The extreme form of this view says *"Esse est percepi"*—to be is to be perceived. This is the "form" of *The Homing Pigeons*.

POTENTIA: The name given to the presumed sub-quantum world by Dr. Werner Heisenberg. Space and time do not exist in *potentia;* but all the phenomena of the space-time manifold emerge from *potentia*. Compare with HIDDEN VARIABLE and INFORMATION.

QUANTUM: An entity whose energies occur in discrete lumps— e.g., photons are the quanta of the electromagnetic field. Quanta have both wave and particle aspects, the wave aspect being the probability of detecting the particle at a certain place and time.

QUANTUM LOGIC: A system of symbolic logic not restricted to the "either it's A or it's not-A" choices of Aristotelian logic. Chiefly due to Dr. John von Neumann and Dr. David Finkelstein, this approach evades the paradoxes of other interpretations of quantum mechanics by assuming that the universe is multi-valued, not two-valued; Dr. Finkelstein expresses this by saying "In addition to a *yes* and a *no,* the universe contains a *maybe*." See EIGENSTATE.

QUANTUM MECHANICS: The mathematical system for describing the atomic and subatomic realm. There is no dispute about how to *do* quantum mechanics—i.e., calculate the probabilities within this realm. All the controversy is about what the quantum mechanics equations imply about reality, which is known as the *interpretation* of quantum mechanics. The principal lines of interpretation are the Copenhagen Interpretation and/or Non-Objectivity and/or Bell's Theorem and/or Non-Locality and/or the Everett-Wheeler-Graham multi-worlds model.

QUIP: The quantum inseparability principle. An acronym coined by Dr. Nick Herbert to refer to the non-locality implicit in the Einstein-Rosen-Podolsky argument and explicit in Bell's Theorem.

STATE VECTOR: The mathematical expression describing one of *two or more* states that a quantum system can be in; for instance, an electron can be in either of two spin states, called "spin up" and "spin down." The amusing thing about quantum mechanics is that each state vector can be regarded as the superposition of other state vectors.

SUPERDETERMINISM: The approach to quantum theory urged by Dr. Fritjof Capra in *The Tao of Physics*. This interpretation rejects "contrafactual definiteness"; that is, it assumes that any statements about what *could have* happened are meaningless. A consequence of this view is that all distinction between observer and observed, or self and universe, also becomes meaningless; I had no choice about writing this book, Pocket Books had no choice about publishing it, and you had no choice about reading it, since there is only one thing happening and we are all seamlessly welded into it.

SYNCHRONICITY: A term introduced by psychologist Dr. Carl Jung and physicist Dr. Wolfgang Pauli to describe connections, or meaningful "coincidences," that do not make sense in terms of cause-and-effect. It is thought by some that such connections may indicate the Hidden Variable at work or some sort of non-local Information System.

VON NEUMANN'S CATASTROPHE: More fully, Von Neumann's catastrophe of the infinite regress. A demonstration by Dr. John Von Neumann that quantum mechanics entails an infinite regress of measurements before the quantum uncertainty can be removed. That is, any measuring device is itself a quantum system containing uncertainty; a second measuring device, used to monitor the first, contains its own quantum uncertainty; and so on, to infinity. Wigner and others have pointed out that this uncertainty is only terminated by the decision of the experimenter. Compare NEURO-.